For Laurie, Reese, and Phoenix

Always

Special thanks to:

Mom, Dad, Jordy, Kirsten, Luke, Nate, Nicky,

and especially Trina L and Allana H

For teaching resources visit:

sites.google.com/view/trmnovella

"From now on it is only through a conscious choice and through a deliberate policy that humanity can survive."

-Pope John Paul II

"You have a choice. Live or die. Every breath is a choice. Every minute is a choice. To be or not to be."

-Chuck Palahniuk

"Ojibwe prophecy speaks of a time during the seventh fire when our people will have a choice between two paths. The first path is well-worn and scorched. The second path is new and green. It is our choice as communities and as individuals how we will proceed."

-Winona LaDuke

"When I let go of what I am, I become what I might be."

-Lao Tzu

Chapter 1

In the darkness, a silver razor glistens as it moves towards its target: a man with no name. He can't move, strapped to the chair in this strange and unknown place. Time slows as he can sense every minuscule variation in the room. A drop of water forms on the ceiling, an air current from the fans flows over him, a tiny insect begins to flutter its wings. The thoughts begin to race through his mind at hyperspeed in comparison to the room almost frozen in time.

  The blade inches closer to his neck, but he isn't sure if this is what he wants anymore. Was he willing to give up everything that he'd ever known? He can feel the blade begin to pierce his skin. In a moment of hesitation, he cries out for it to stop. Is this the right decision? He needs an answer. Why is he here? How did he get here? What would happen next? Was everything all a lie? He takes a deep breath. This decision could affect all of humanity. He knows what he needs to do, but he isn't sure if he is strong enough to do it.

Chapter 2

People pack the oval shaped stadium to the ceiling, stretching several levels above the playing surface. Everyone comes to watch, to witness. This is the event everyone lives for. There is not an empty seat in the house. The excitement can be felt throughout the stadium. The buzz of the crowd slowly fades away as the players emerge from tunnels opening onto a grass field below.

On the field players are lined at either end of the oval, each team in a tight formation. Each team is familiar to the other, but that won't make it any less exciting, in fact it adds to the intensity of the game. A horn sounds to start the action. A purple ball the size of a cantaloupe materializes in the middle of the pitch.

On either side the players begin to spread out from the crowd to be seen on every side of the stadium. One team is dressed in blue, the standard armor thick enough to provide some protection, but thin enough to allow them to move with speed and agility. Helmets follow the contours of their heads, a clear visor covering their eyes. On the other side of the field, the blue is traded with red, similar armour, only slightly different for different shapes of bodies and different sizes. Six players move on either side, both men and women but there is no distinguishable difference between the two. In this game there are no positions but strategy is everything; one miscalculation could cost the game, one wrong move would cost a life.

The object of the game is simple: get the ball to the other side of the playing field. However, to accomplish this, each team must work together on offence and defence at the same time, carefully constructing a plan of attack. The rules are few, but the ways to play are infinite.

Walls begin to form on either side on the playing field, creating small barriers. Blue walls surround the blue players as red walls are constructed at the other end. From above it looks like a maze of two colours gradually moving towards each other. As the walls meet in the middle, they start to fall. Players from either side run through the pathways created in their colour. The battle rolls back and forth, one team moving forward, then the other pushing back. Neither team gains much ground, but the arena is littered with the debris from fallen barriers.

Suddenly one of the blue players emerges from behind their defensive protection. He begins sprinting towards the ball in the middle of the pitch quickly snatching it up. Almost instantly, a wall erupts in front of him, but he anticipates this and dodges to the right. The red team senses his anticipation and walls are up on either side of him. He sends the ball flying over his shoulder. Another blue player jumps and catches the ball as ascending metal plates form under his feet. He steps off each plate as it falls to the ground allowing him to climb higher and higher. Columns of blue concrete start to rise under his feet, taking him above the crowd.

Red players start to climb the columns on either side. This is one of the riskiest plays in this game as a blue player is at the height of the stadium and there are no safety cords. This move also leaves a large obstacle in the middle of the field, a pyramid of blue and red concrete columns.

How the red team reacts could determine the course of this game. The safe move is to put a barrier where he is headed and make him alter his course or halt it. The players know that this decision will either win them the game or lose it. They choose the more dangerous option. The columns continue to rise and start cracking as steel balls crash into the columns immediately after they rise up from the ground. The blue player has experienced this before but that doesn't stop him from stumbling and he slips, descending nearly 100 feet below. The crowd gasps. A bar appears in the air and he grabs it with his hand as he falls, but in the process the ball comes free and drops to the ground below. The crowd cheers.

One of the other red players starts along the ground, scooping the ball off the ground below the fallen columns. As she runs, blue walls are springing up around her. For every blue wall that blocks her path, there comes up a red platform on a 45 degree angle. She is able to step off each platform and jump in the opposite direction to avoid the blue walls. She crashes as a third wall appears right above her head, the ball rolling free in front of her. She crumples to the ground, motionless, and remains there, still unmoving. A siren blasts and everything on the field remains frozen in time.

The crowd rises to their feet. There is a collective hush as if every person in the audience had inhaled at the same time, holding their breaths. From the side of the stadium, a hole opens and a floating vehicle hovers over top of the motionless red player for a few seconds and then floats back. The player is gone from the field and will not be replaced. The horn sounds and movement resumes on the field. There is an exhale followed by an outburst of cheers as the fans get back into the action.

Once again the blue team gains possession of the ball. This time two blue players run up the field a few feet apart from each other. Instead of walls, large towers begin to blast out of the ground. The whole stadium has risen several feet from the debris of the structures. Platforms are constructed so the players can traverse the rubble below them.

This is a crucial point in the game where the blue team has an extra player that will allow them more opportunities for an offensive maneuver. One blue player is slightly behind the first one, both running full speed. The first player with the ball stops, pivots, and tosses the ball backwards. The second player cuts right as she receives the ball from the first player. Then, without the ball, the first player continues to spin and veers left. Pillars of blue spring up on either side and the blue player with the ball bounces from side to side, planting his foot to spring on each pillar.

The second player in blue continues to climb the air as three enemies emerge from behind their defenses. They converge on the blue player with the ball, each dodging newly erected towers. The closest one in red dives at the ball carrier. Dodging the tackle, blue springs forward into a roll over the red player as he slams into the blue walls. Another red player lunges forward, hitting the blue player in the upper body and the third red player hits her legs, sending her into a vertical spin. As she is about to hit the ground, another blue player comes out from behind one of the blue walls where he was hidden. As if in slow motion, the player with the ball tosses the ball up as she continues spinning upside down. The new blue player grabs the ball out of the air and dodges past the fallen players. He squeezes between two red walls, steps onto a blue plate at waist level and launches himself forward, flipping over another red tower. He crashes into the green barrier on the other side and everything goes silent.

A different horn sounds and the crowd erupts with screaming and applause. The game is over. The blue team has won and the red team suffered one casualty, a minor loss with major repercussions. It is a game, however, few things are considered more serious in this world.

Chapter 3

Begin transmission: accessing file, History of War.

A video hologram pops up and a woman's voice can be heard over the images. "The History of War as told by Elder 105 2117. Since the beginning of the human race, humanity has been defined by the ugliness of violence." As the woman speaks, images pop up: men holding little pointed sticks in their hands. The voice continues, "Humans created weapons at first to survive against the wild creatures of the planet. Later those weapons were turned against each other over possessions, territory, and power." Images of the humans start to evolve and the little forms start attacking each other. Piles of bodies start to stack up, forming a pile of corpses. "As human intelligence grew so did the capacity for destruction. Weapons became more efficient in taking life."

Humans with guns are seen being mowed down by gunfire. Another row replaces the first. A plane flies over top, dropping little pellets falling below exploding into clouds of dust, fire, and blood. "The First World War was fought over power." Little men in trenches can be seen shooting at each other. "The Second World War was fought over hate." A man stands in front of a crowd and raises his arm in the air. Tanks roll through towns made of rubble. Bodies are burned by the hundreds. Skeletons are marched into camps for the dead. "The Third World War was the war of terror and lies." Screens pop up showing reporters with explosions in the background. A man stands behind a podium, a flag waving behind him. Planes fly over top and everything is destroyed. Once beautiful cities turn to ashes. "The Fourth World War was over money. This was when all currency was abolished." Hordes of tiny figures converge on giant fortresses. Rows are cut down, but they are quickly replaced by others from behind as they overtake the fortresses. Piles of bills are set on fire in the streets; coins are melted into liquid metal. "The Fifth World War was over technology. It saw the most carnage and almost wiped humanity out altogether." Soldiers surround a walled city, enormous creatures emerge from behind them, all attacking the walls. Large explosions start to erupt outside of the walls, sending body parts, both human and non-human, flying in the air. This continues until nothing is left outside of the walls.

"The weapons had become so efficient at destroying life that almost none was left. It was called The Final War. Those who survived all vowed they would never see it happen again." Images of people sitting around a table pop up, a document is passed from person to person, men and women each press their finger onto the screen one at a time. A single drop of blood from the finger being collected, not only to symbolize the pledge of no more bloodshed but also to bind them in ways not even all of them would know. The hologram fades. "This began the Age of Peace and humanity has prospered ever since."

End transmission.

Chapter 4

The Chip

In the late 32nd century, technology development had reached its zenith with the implementation of thought recognition. The first use was to control communication devices to transmit thoughts directly. People no longer needed external devices to communicate, it could be done directly through controlled thought processes.

With the combination of 3D printing and matter transportation, people were able to create almost anything they could imagine, right before their eyes. As the technology became faster, items could be constructed almost instantly. The major issue became the use of resources. As the world reached the pinnacle of human population at 20 billion, natural resources were growing scarce. The divide between the rich and poor grew every day, with the vast majority of the world living in extreme poverty.

World War 4 saw the oppressed and impoverished mount a rebellion against those with all the power. The result was mass destruction of life and property. The rebels had the numbers to keep attacking, but they could not overwhelm the defenses in all places. This uprising, however, led to the research of the most powerful technology humanity had ever known. The Thought Recognition Microchip or TRM combined all the modern technology to allow an individual to make something appear from mere thought. The only limitations were rare resources, food, and living matter. Matter transportation required the matter to be reduced to individual molecules and living matter would never survive the reconstruction, no matter how many different methods were tried. Food was possible, but it never tasted quite right and there were serious health concerns associated with reconstructed foods.

World War 5 was fought over control of the TRM. A small group of the most wealthy had created enough Microchips to have a small army. Those trying to steal the TRM technology turned to biochemical attacks as they could not do anything against the

TRM controlled army. This led to a variety of biochemical mutations that became a terror to both sides. The TRM army built an impenetrable fortress and left the attackers to perish trying to defend against their own abominable creations. Several nuclear attacks from both sides wiped out most of the mutations along with the majority of humanity that was fighting outside of the TRM walled city. For the first time in many millennia, the human population was reduced to less than 1 million. The Treaty of Vienna was signed at the Wiener Staatsoper, pledging an end to war, biochemical weapons, and protection of the TRM technology.

Chapter 5

Life inside of the walled fortress, known as New Europe, became regimented, but it was necessary to have peace and happiness.

After several generations had passed, memories of the old ways faded away and the new way was just how it was. Everything was made as equal as humanly possible. Everyone lived in the same type of living quarters, a modest three room abode of 750 square feet. It contained a sleeping room, a living room, and a kitchen. Food and supplies were distributed on a weekly rations basis. Each person was given what they needed so no one was left wanting and no one had too much. Waste was almost non-existent as the TRM measured energy intake and expenditure so exact allotments could be sent for each person. It took many years to perfect these calculations, but they were as close as they would get now.

Every year after the age of 14, members were assigned a task for either one or two years, depending on the demand for that task. For example, year 15 was a simple task of yard and lawn maintenance throughout all of New Europe. Year 16 was public area cleaning. Years 28-29 were the most dreaded years of sewage and waste treatment.

To regulate the number of children born each year, procreation was the task of those in years 23 and 24. This was seen by all as the most idyllic years as it was a break from the usual menial tasks in other years. The TRM was able to regulate fertility to only those two years. Men and women were assigned a partner based on their genetic makeup. This process had allowed the most useful dominant traits to permeate humanity. It made most people look similar with brown eyes, brown hair, and a medium dark skin tone. Each group born together was referred to as a gen based on their birth number. There was the odd variation in each gen, but even the men and women had similar features.

Disease and birth defects were even more rare and were dealt with discreetly and humanely. Birth was one of the few natural things left in society. They tried using technology to manage it, but the results were less than desirable.

Each pair had two children, one each year of procreation, which kept the population stable. Each year there would be a few twins, but they were usually offset by those unable to conceive. Most diseases had been eradicated; birth defects were commonly detected after conception and genetically fixed before birth. Murder was an extreme rarity. The main cause of death, outside of deployment, was falling during training activities. In most cases, the majority of a gen would live to their full life expectancy of 80.

After birth, the babies were taken to the infant care centre where they were nourished by those in year 40. They would never know their parents and their parents would never know them. This made attachment a non-issue, but every so often two people would feel a connection and wonder for a second what it was.

Some partners ended up continuing a relationship after the procreation years, but it was more the exception than the norm. Since no one had specific parents, the old concept of family had been completely lost. Those in the same gen tended to bond like brothers and sisters. Since there were no child-rearing responsibilities, relationships tended to be more fluid. It caused the odd conflict, but most people accepted this as the norm. The lack of familial ties allowed for easy transitions between each change of year. For the deployment, each person someone might be attached to would be deploying as well. This also meant that each member would be fighting to protect their brother or sister while deployed and there would not be the worry for those back home.

The TRM was inserted in babies 3 days after birth. Many different ages had been tested, but 3 days proved the most optimal time. In the adult years there was a greater chance of rejection, which usually resulted in death or severe psychological damage after an extended amount of time. Teenage years were not much better, with a greater chance of survival, but still severe side effects. Age 3 was the worst as more than half of that gen was wiped out and had to be replaced by other gens. It was a quick and seamless procedure. At 3 days the babies were able to recover within a week and were back to normal before the first month, with casualties less than 1%.

Children were raised in the communal educational centre or CEC. They lived here from birth to age fifteen. At the age of fifteen, a person became an official contributing member of society and was given a number indicating their year of entry and their place within that year. Each year had up to 9999 members and the latest year of entry was at 475. So the first member would be 475 0001, but would just be referred to as 1 within their gen. At the CEC they would train how to use their TRM by those most experienced in years 55-59. The benefit of the TRM was that basic knowledge and information could be uploaded as fast as the brain could process it. The real education was teaching children how to use their Chip. It was a long process requiring patience, but by year 14, over 90% of the gen would be completely proficient in all basic uses of the TRM. Those that failed the final test would receive another year of training. For just under 3%, a second failure resulted in specialized training.

Each year, some of the top performers were retained to train and supervise the new gen coming in to replace them. After year 60, members served on the governing committee, but most would spend most of their time either assisting a gen of their choice or in the relaxing areas. No one lived past age 80. Population control made sure that there were enough members in each gen to perform each job. It was a careful act balancing each gen with unexpected deaths or extended illnesses. Multiple deaths were rare, usually only in the extremely rare case of an outbreak. The TRM has toxin detectors that cover almost all serious diseases, but the odd new strain would slip through every so often. Most gens would suffer less than a hundred deaths in the lifespan of that gen. Deployment was the exception with some gens experiencing major losses. After two years of deployment, there was a rebalancing year that blended gens to adjust for any significant losses a gen may have suffered.

Chapter 6

Member 445 3378 stands in a field. Bricks start stacking about ten feet in front of him, forming a circular structure. The structure rises to a height of twelve feet and a diameter of six. *Download instructions for RPG. Download instructions for transparent shield.* A handle appears in 3378's hand, with a long metal cylinder forming on the handle, one end resting on his shoulder. A rocket forms in the other end of the barrel. Pointing it towards the brick structure, he pulls the trigger and the rocket flies into the middle, exploding on impact, sending bricks in every direction. Some debris flies backwards, but stops in front of 3378, as if hitting an invisible barrier.

Incoming transmission from 403 0011.

A projection of an older woman pops up in 3378's vision. "Sorry to disturb your training, 445 3378. There have been reports of volatile activity in sector Y0W. We are moving deployment for all 445s up seven months. All 445s will begin pre-transition in two weeks. We apologize for this inconvenience. An adjustment will be made during the relaxation year."

End transmission.

3378 lays down the RPG as the rubble from the destroyed tower begins to disappear. He did not look forward to deployment, but anything was better than sewage and waste management. That must have been why the deployment years were right after. That way it seemed more desirable. They had all seen the video footage of the world outside of the walls and run the simulations, but it was the stories that made it something to fear. They ranged from ridiculous to horrifying. One said that less than half of each year returned from deployment and they were replaced by automatons that looked and socialized exactly like them. Before deployment everyone was scanned and their automaton was made in case they didn't return. Few believed any part of that. On the other end there were tales of biochemical mutations that had continued to evolve and breed into deadly monsters the size of a small housing unit. This was slightly more believable despite the history records downplaying the threat of these creatures. Why else would they stay inside the walls? Why would they have all of this weapon training if using weapons to attack a human was prohibited?

The field flickers for a second. It is brief, almost unnoticeable, but you can recognize it after enough time in the simulators. No program is perfect, and the most minor flaw can be seen in a minute variation.

He could only remember one instance in his life when he saw someone try to attack another person with a weapon. One of the supervisors in his 18th year lost it on 445 0001 and went after him with a scythe they were using to cut the long grass. Most 1s were obnoxious because of their popularity, but he didn't see what happened in this case and he didn't mind the 1 in their gen most of the time. The supervisor ran straight at him screaming and holding the blade in the air. He came within inches of striking 1, who crouched in a ball with his hands over his head. Then the older man just froze. His eyes were still moving frantically, but every other muscle of his body was paralyzed. The police were there in less than a minute to take him away. 3378 never knew where he went or what happened to him. It was one of the few strange moments in his life that he could recall.

3378 looks around. The only thing left is the scorch marks in the ground left by the explosion. He turns around and a door appears in the air. He steps through and travels from an open field to a street in the middle of a city. The simulation rooms are well kept. There will be no traces of his training by the time the next member uses the room.

Chapter 7

There are only two types of transports in New Europe: the
Individual Transport Module (ITM) and the Large Group Transport
(LGT) used for deployments. Every member receives an individual
transport at year 19. They are only operational within the walls of
New Europe.

     Member 455 7042 steps up to the Individual Transport
Module or ITM. She hesitates before stepping through the
vertically open door to the transport. It is her first time flying. All of
the instructions have been downloaded and processed. In her
mind she has flown over a thousand times, but the simulations
never accurately create the sense of fear of death. 42 takes a
deep breath and reaches her foot and arms forward, pulling
herself up into the seat. Leaning forward, she drops her chest into
the harness and places her feet into the footholds at the back.
She is horizontal on her stomach, her legs bent below her and her
arms holding onto the handles just under her chin. There are
manual controls in case the thought controls fail, but those
controls were rarely used.

     The ITM slowly lifts off the ground, bobbing to one side
and then the other. After a few bumps it levels out, hovering in the
air about four feet off the ground. She is floating in the middle of
an empty street near her housing unit. The training instructions
told her to start with a straight narrow path to learn speed and
balance. Navigational devices were installed, but each member
needed to know how to control the ITM both manually and through
the TRM. She thinks about moving to the end of the street and the
ITM takes off like a bullet shot from a high-powered sniper rifle. It
took 42 by surprise as she was thrown backwards in her harness.
She keeps her hands on the manual steering handles, the
muscles in her arms straining to hold on. The ITM gently slows
and descends towards the ground. 42 lands and pries her fingers
from the grips. Her legs are locked, and she has to get out
gingerly to stretch them out.

     Okay, I got this she says to herself. Strapping back in, she
feels more confident now that she knows what to expect. This

time the ITM lifts up steadily and starts moving forward at a moderate pace. As the street curves, so does the ITM. She maneuvers left and right, dodging buildings like a fly avoiding humans at a garden party. Her confidence builds and she becomes more daring. *Let's try the manual mode* she thinks. *Disconnect TRM* she thinks and the ITM drops, plummeting to the ground. *Oh crap.* She is about to engage the TRM again when her training kicks in and she pulls back on the handles and the ITM veers back up, coming a few feet from a fatal collision with the ground.

Confidence had always been 42's strength and often her weakness. She likes the feeling of being in control and decides to do some free flying over the forest. The forest inside the walls is still massive and gorgeous, rows of dark green lime trees and turquoise lakes. She glides over the water, so close that the jetstream from the ITM ripples the water underneath. It reminds her of Central Park from New York City, back in the 25th century, before the city collapsed in the Fourth World War. 42 spent many hours of her free time browsing through the ancient history of civilization. It fascinated her how cities had formed all over the world from nothing. Now the only way to experience those cities was in the simulators. All she had ever actually seen with her own eyes was inside these walls. Gliding over the trees and water made her feel alive, like she could be anywhere in the world at that moment. The sun is shining, which means her ITM could run forever. She soars high above the trees, catching a glimpse of the world beyond the walls. The beauty of the sight moves her to tears.

She is starting to come down when she hears a bang from behind her and the ITM starts to shake. *Engage TRM,* she thinks immediately. *Emergency repair.* The ITM has lost control and the TRM is not able to regain it. It starts to spiral to her right. She is heading past the wall. She frantically pulls at the manual controls, but nothing works as she continues to plummet. She works through every emergency protocol as she starts to skim the tree tops. *At least I'll get to finally go beyond the wall before I die.*

Chapter 8

445 3378 is cleaning the waste at the edge of the forest when he hears the loud bang. He looks up to see smoke trailing from an ITM, which is headed over the wall. Something is wrong he thinks. No one travels over the wall in an ITM, let alone a smoking one. He looks around to see if someone else had spotted it and is going to do something. He sees no one, not even the Wall Patrol that would normally be up there. *Someone must have seen it.* He goes back to his work, but his conscience starts to kick in and gnaw at him. He throws down his shovel and runs to the wall. Never has he really thought about actually going over the walls, stepping on the outside. Now, he doesn't have time to think, he just acts.

Steps start popping out of the wall as 3378 runs up them. He has done this a million times, but not to this height. The wall is 100 feet high. It was built as protection, but now it keeps everyone in as well. He reaches the top and looks out for the first time in his life. He had seen videos and knew what to expect but seeing it with his own eyes is so much more fantastic. A sea of green covers the landscape. A small river carves through the trees. The clouds look like they are painted with whites and greys in the orange sky. Looking out, he forgets why he had come up there. The tail of smoke from the trees reminds him why and brings him out of his daze.

He makes steps down the outside of the wall. As he descends, he thinks about the consequences of going outside of the wall without permission. Surely the tribunal would see that it was an emergency and he was only trying to help. He knew the punishments for transgressions were harsh, but never really knew what happened in the administrative offices. It didn't matter now, he had crossed the threshold and was not turning back.

He hits the ground. It feels softer outside. He runs towards the smoke spiral, barely visible through the tree brush. As he closes in on it, he notices the sounds around him, like music he has never heard before. Little whooshes and whistles, chirps and cracks. Inside the walls it sounds so dead compared to this. All of his life he had only seen holograms of the outside world and videos of the past. Now, experiencing it with his own senses is overwhelming. He had always imagined it to be a scary place, full of biochems ready to eat him.

He makes his way to the base of the smoke. The ITM is trapped in the branches halfway up the tree. Metal spikes jab into the trunk of the tree and 3378 grabs a hold of them to begin his ascent. As he climbs, he looks up at his target. The ITM looks stable, but he doesn't know about the person inside of it. It is high in the tree and if it fell, no one would survive that crash.

It was just over a year ago that he worked in vehicle repair and knew the weaknesses of the ITMs. They were designed for short distance travel and quick maneuverability, but could make long distances, if pushed. They had the best collision detection design possible, which allowed for a thinner protective exterior. In turn, this meant that any failure of the collision detection system could lead to a fatal crash. They were also equipped with an auto-shutoff if they ever went past the wall.

He climbs as quickly as he can, adding in extra holds as needed. 3378 looked like most other New Europeans, same skin tone, same brown hair, same brown eyes, but he was always slightly shorter than everyone else in his gen. It usually put him at a disadvantage, but it did give him an edge in things like climbing and fitting into small spaces.

When he gets to the branch that the ITM is on, he pauses to survey the damage. No signs of movement inside. There is not a visible flame causing the smoke. As he eases out onto the branch, the whole tree creaks and the ITM shifts. He waits until it stops again. He starts to make stabilizing supports on either side, bracing with the other main tree limbs. When he is sure it is safe enough, he moves out to the ITM and peers in the window. He sees a girl unconscious in the cockpit. He taps the manual door opener and it pops open; the stabilizers keep it from moving this time. He reaches in, releases the restraints, and pulls the girl out of the seat and onto the branch. With no time to waste, he makes a gentle slide to the ground, winding between the branches. He holds her in his arms and goes down the slide.

Sliding down reminds him of his early education. He would see how high he could get and make the slide with the most twists possible. This was how he spent every afternoon of free time until his teacher told him to stop. *We can make so many things,* she said, *but we can't make another one of you. You need to be more careful or you will get hurt. No more slides.* And he stopped making slides after that.

At the bottom, he lies the girl on the ground. She has hair slightly darker than his, cut to just brush her shoulders. Her skin is the same tone as his, but nearly flawless. When he lifts up her eyelids, he sees the greenest eyes he has ever seen. They remind him of the jewel in the Last Museum of Mankind. He had thought it was so strange that people valued pieces of metal, glass, and paper, but the way that jewel shone made him want it more than anything. Her pulse is faint, but it is a sign of life at least. He had done all of the basic medical training in the firefighting year and had downloaded all of the protocols. No signs of trauma, no visible wounds or broken bones. She must have hit her head.

He is checking her head for some sign of injury when he hears the hum of the LGT and the pounding of the footsteps. *Finally, some help has arrived. Took long enough,* he thinks.

"Stand up slowly. Hands where we can see them. Don't attempt to use your Chip or things will be much worse than they already are." It is the voice of a man. One he has never heard before, but it sounds like the drill sergeant he had seen in videos about deployment a few times. He stands up slowly as instructed and turns to face the man. There are several others, all in the deployment uniform, all with weapons pointed at him. Two move around him to go to the girl.

"She's hurt. I got her out of her ITM. I don't-"

"Quiet. Don't say another word," the man snaps. The other two men pick up the girl and carry her towards the LGT which has landed in a clearing just visible beyond the trees.

"But-"

"Not. One. Word."

Chapter 9

3378 is led down a long dark hallway. The men had taken him to a holding cell the other night. They didn't say anything to him and he was too afraid to ask any questions. The hallway opens up to a large room filled with rows of people on either side and a giant screen in the front. The man and woman leading him bring him to a seat near the middle of the room. Most people in the room are looking at him, some with concern, some with contempt. He knew what this place was, but never thought he would be here. The usual proceeding for a breach of the city limits was a tribunal with the current year supervisors. Where he was headed was reserved for the most serious offenses. *What do they think happened?*

A man's face appears on the screen. "411 0001 reporting for jurisdiction. Please stand 445 3378. You have been charged with leaving the city limits without clearance and actions leading to the death of a city member. Do you deny these charges?" the man asks in a monotone voice, showing a blatant disinterest in the proceedings.

"Yes! What is happening? Who died?" 3378 yells as one of his escorts moves towards him.

The man on the screen keeps talking, ignoring his questions. "Can we hear from the witness?"

The man that threatened him in the forest steps forward from the audience and faces the screen. "Member 438 5124, Chief Tactical Officer, witness to the incident. We were alerted to two individuals outside of the city limits. One had a malfunctioning ITM and crash landed in the woods to the northeast. When we arrived on the scene, member 445 3378 was on top of member 455 7042. He appeared to have removed her from the ITM and brought her to the ground via a constructed slide. It was not clear what he was doing. My men removed member 455 7042 who died shortly after from trauma suffered during the crash and possibly exacerbated by the heroics of member 445 3378."

"What? What are you saying?" 3378 yells, standing up.

The guard pushes him down by his shoulder and whispers in his ear, "I wouldn't try that again. Do you not know where you are?"

"Member 445 3378. You may now speak in your defense. However, I warn you that each outburst is recorded on your personal history. Choose your words carefully." The man on the screen changes his tone so slightly that most would not notice.

"I saw the ITM go over the wall. I was cleaning the sewage pipe in area H8. I didn't see anyone else, so I climbed the wall to go help." There was a gasp in the crowd. He continues, "When I got to the crash site, I saw the ITM in the tree and I climbed up. I saw the girl and she was unconscious, so I got her out before the ITM hit the ground. I used a slide to get her out as fast as I knew how. I was trying to save her. I didn't see any trauma. She had a pulse when I checked her. I don't know what happened to her. I suspected she had hit her head, but she was alive when they took her." He starts speaking frantically as he finishes his version of what happened.

"So you do not deny going over the wall without permission. And you do not deny moving an injured member. Is there anyone else that wishes to speak on this case?" The man seems almost bored.

"I didn't kill her!" 3378 shouts. This time a jolt of electricity stabs into his side and his knees buckle, folding him into his seat.

"Speak out of line one more time 3378 and you will be removed!" For the first time, the man on the screen showed some emotion, clearly annoyed by his yelling. Those in the government rarely use short form names.

"I have one suggestion, if I may," says 438 5124. "In two weeks, the accused is to begin preparation for early deployment. We can use all of the members we can get to deal with a situation in the outer lands. I suggest we delay judgement until after he returns from deployment. Perhaps his duty in deployment will offer some redemption or serve justice on its own." *What did he mean by that?*

"A wise suggestion. Agreed. Judgement of member 445 3378 will be delayed until his return from deployment. Until that time he will be under surveillance. Court adjourned." The man's face disappears from the screen, like he had somewhere else he needed to be.

The guard that shocked 3378 grabs him by the arm and pulls him back out into the hallway.

"What just happened? Don't I get to defend myself?" 3378 asks.

"You did. And what just happened is that you got a second chance in life. Most don't get that. My advice is don't screw it up." That is all the guard says as he herds 3378 back down the hall and out of the building.

Chapter 10

The night is dark, the dawn waiting just around the corner. The cool night breeze slips through the grass, whispering between the blades. He walks towards the clearing, seeing a shape on the ground in the distance. It is someone he knows but doesn't know. A loud crack thunders over his head and he looks up to see a ship crashing down through the trees toward him. He jumps to the side as it lands inches away from him. When he turns back to the body in the grass, it is gone. He looks around and feels the darkness closing in on him like a cloak being wrapped over his head. A girl's voice drifts faintly from the trees around the clearing. Spinning, he tries to pinpoint where it is coming from. He can't make out the words. Then it comes in crisper and louder. "You have to get away."

3378 bolts up in his bed. The image of the girl's face is left in his mind. He is sure it was the voice of the girl from the crash, even though he never heard her speak. His room is quiet like the holding cell, but the air feels different. It is his home and it feels right. That feeling of home didn't take away the cold shiver he got from what happened the other day and the eerie feeling of the dream. There were so many questions that he wanted answered, but no one to ask them to. He was either very lucky or very unlucky, he couldn't decide which it was though. Nothing could be done about it right now; he had to prepare for deployment.

Everyone always looked forward to the deployment years with nervous excitement. They were finally let out of their giant concrete prison and allowed to see the outside world, breathe the open air and see the horizon. Since 3378 already had this experience, he wasn't quite as excited as he was before. Deployment usually saw a 10% decrease in each gen upon return. This is why there was a rebalancing year after, where some were placed into adjacent years to fill all of the occupational spots. The decrease fluctuated from year to year, but there was always a decrease. When he was younger, he remembered hearing about the year where only one member returned. There were many stories about what happened. Some said they went mad and turned on each other, others said they were attacked by biochems, and a quieter rumor was that their chips malfunctioned, killing them all. 3378 was never one to believe such stories, but it still made a person pause. Behind every story was a thread of truth.

He goes in and out of the cleaning station next to his bedroom, puts on his clothes, and eats the morning rations that were delivered at the same time as always. The farms provided quality food and the TRM calculated the exact amount that he needed, but it never felt like quite enough. He slips on his shoes and walks through the front door. His ITM appears on the pad in front of the housing unit. 1001 people from his year live in this housing unit, 3000-3999 plus their current supervisor. Each person has their own unit and they all share one communal recreation area, which has all the activities that members enjoy.

The recreational area is divided into the physical training section, an arts section, and the recreational simulators. 3378 didn't spend a lot of time there, but when he did, he enjoyed the ancient aerial battle simulations where he would pilot an Albatros fighter plane and try to gun down anyone in his path. Most people couldn't handle the spinning of the flight simulation, but it never really bothered 3378.

His ITM glides down the street, through the other housing units. ITMs are zipping by on either side. There are never collisions with other ITMs because of the built-in sensors. Even in manual control, an ITM will avoid a crash. He always felt safe and free when he was flying. When he saw the girl go over the wall, it was the first time he saw an ITM crash. It makes him rethink his sense of security as he glides to the training centre.

He steps out of the ITM and is greeted by his supervisor, 421 3347. He is an older man with a gruff look, but a kind heart. "I heard what happened. I'm sorry you had to go through that. It was stupid to go over the wall, but it sounds like you were trying to do the right thing," the man says as he puts his hand on 3378's shoulder. He was as close to a father as 3378 would ever have.

"Thanks. I don't even really know what happened. Do you know about the girl? Is she dead?"

"From what I have been told, yes, she is. Her ITM malfunctioned and hit the trees. They said that the impact of the crash caused internal trauma that could not be reversed by the medical centre."

"But it doesn't make sense. The ITMs are designed to withstand greater impacts than that and she was alive when I found her. They just rushed her away without even checking her. Why didn't they ask me what happened?"

"I learned a long time ago not to ask too many questions. They usually lead to answers that you don't want to know. Once you come back from deployment, this should all be blown over. Get inside, the hand-to-hand combat training has already started."

3378 walks into the training centre and finds his group of 3300's. He blends into the group which is working on boxing techniques. Each member has preloaded the instructions for each form of combat. It is just a matter of putting that knowledge into physical training. He could never comprehend how people used to learn information by reading books. He enjoyed looking at them in the Last Museum, but it seemed like such a painstakingly time-consuming process of gaining knowledge. The Chip made everything in life easier and instantaneous. Almost anything you wanted could be accessed with a simple thought pattern. 3378 had never been in an actual fight, but he knew over 1000 ways to attack and hurt someone as well as defend himself from such an attack.

After the individual training, the groups pair up for some sparring. The 3300's were against the 0's. 3378 knew this would be a challenge as the 0's in every year always thought they were better than the rest and constantly tried to prove it. What's worse is that his procreation partner is in that group. They usually got along well during the two years of procreation, but she would tease him when anyone else was around. She was 445 0009 and everyone called her 9, like they called him 3378. However, she would call him 8, both to build him up and to mock him. He had developed real feelings for her, but after year 24 ended, she never said more than "hey" to him. Any thoughts he had of continuing their relationship quickly fell apart. She was cordial with him, but nothing more.

He was next up to spar and he saw 9 cutting in line on the other side. Was she trying to fight against him? Another funny thing about the past was this idea that women were weaker than men. The concept of inequality had disappeared long ago. There was little difference between men and women now outside of reproductive organs. Even appearances were almost identical in many cases. Sparring with a woman was not an issue, but why did it have to be her? He wanted to hold her, not punch her in the face. Did she really hate him that much?

The bell rings and the previous fighter is helped through the ropes of the sparring ring, severely bruised and holding what looks like a broken arm. 3378 steps to the side to let him by and then enters the ring. He walks up to 9 to give the usual greeting of a double tap of the back of the hands. As they approach, 9 says loudly, "Hey 8, long time no see." He is about to give a witty retort when she leans in closer as they tap hands and whispers, "I heard what happened. I have something to tell you." She backs away as the bell rings. *What is she talking about?*

The only rule of sparring was that a member could not use their Chip to aid in the battle. All TRMs were disabled during training. This training was intended to prepare members in the event of a Chip malfunction or electromagnetic pulse. Most members relied on their Chip too much and had trouble functioning normally without using it. Simple things like walking up a flight of stairs could be accomplished by creating a gradually rising platform with the Chip. Instead of getting up to grab a tool, another one could be created in seconds. Most members cared little about waste as all created items would be broken back down and harvested to add back to the resource bank. The resource levels and usage were constantly being monitored and controlled, but for the most part members were free to make any little thing they desired. Can't find an item of clothing, just make a new one.

Bam! 9 lands a sucker punch to 3378's stomach while he is daydreaming. She knees him in the head and sends him flying across the ring. "Are you going to fight or just stand there 8?" she goads him. He stands up and prepares his fighting stance. His plan is to practice his dodges and counter moves. He doesn't want to hurt her. She lunges at his head with her foot and he leans to the side, her foot narrowly missing his chin. She brings her leg down on his thigh and he grimaces in pain. Her elbow comes flying at his head and he is just able to roll forward before it connects. She is really trying to hurt him. A spinning backwards kick heads towards him as he comes out of his roll and he drops onto his stomach to miss it. She immediately leaps on him and pulls his left arm behind his back, pinning him to the floor.

"I only have a few seconds to tell you all I can. I'm going to put you into a choke hold. Pretend you're resisting." Was she crazy? What was she trying to do to him? She grabs him around his neck, but she doesn't put pressure on his neck to actually choke him. "You are not safe, you have to get away. Something isn't right here." He sees his opportunity and grabs her hair, throwing her over top of his head. She lands hard on the other side of the ring and he can tell it hurt. *Good*, he thinks, what was she up to?

She runs at him full speed and tackles him to the ground. He wasn't expecting it and it takes the wind out of him. She jumps on top of him again and talks in a quiet, but rushed tone, "Are you a complete idiot 8? I'm trying to help you. When you get on the outside, run and don't look back. Trust me."

"Why should I trust you?" he asks, feeling the blood starting to pool in his mouth.

"Because I am one of the few people you can." She stands up and falls into a defensive stance. This time he feints a hook with his right arm and lands a jab with his left to her left forearm. She bends in pain and he uses the split-second window to sweep her feet. He lands on her and loops his arm under hers and behind her head.

"Why are you telling me this?"

"Because I care about you, you imbecile. If you don't believe me, find out for yourself. If you can." With that she pushes up with her whole body and sends him into the air. As he falls, she thrusts out with both feet and sends him into the corner. He crumples to the floor, unable to move. She walks over to him. "Remember what I said. Don't be a hero and listen for once." She spits out her own mouthful of blood and walks out of the ring on her own.

He sees the medic coming towards him, there is a slight flicker and then everything goes blurry.

Chapter 11

The LGT's doors open and 3378 follows his group on board. 421 3347 is there, greeting the 3000's as they file in. The three weeks of transition did not really prepare him for what he was entering into. He knew all of the protocols, the strategies, the instructions, and histories. Knowledge was one thing, but actual experience was something else completely. His body shakes under the weight of what is about to happen, anyone who was watching would think he was struggling from his supply pack.

He finds his spot on the LGT. It could fit 1005 people exactly. One for each member of the that section of the gen, two pilots, and three supervisors. 3377 and 3379 strap in on either side of him. He had known them his whole life and considered them his closest friends. They had shared many experiences over the years.

When they were 12, they snuck out of the education centre and built a teepee in the forest where they slept for the night. The next morning a search party found them, lights blazing through the cracks in their shelter. For three weeks they survived confinement by talking to each other and telling stories. He still thinks about the story that 3379 told.

It was about a Greek warrior named Ajax who fought in the Trojan War over 4000 years ago. Ajax dueled Hector, the champion of the Trojan army, on several occasions and held his own. When Achilles, a key Greek warrior, was killed in battle, Ajax coveted his armour, which had been made by the god Hephaestus. Odysseus, who was the cleverest of the Greek soldiers, convinced the army that he deserved the armour. Ajax, angry at the outcome, threw himself on his own sword and died. 3378 was so intrigued by the concept of the Greek gods and how they interacted with the humans. The Greek soldiers also captivated him with their sense of honour and duty. Each was willing to give their life for something they believed in.

The LGT lifts into the air. It was a lot more lumbering than an ITM, but it moves with speed when it gets going. The city starts shrinking as they move towards the wall. This time, flying over the wall feels so different. The trees look like little miniature models from the Last Museum. It doesn't look real, but it is beautiful. The green and blue mix and mingle in contrast with the straight grey lines of the city. He continues to look out the window as the clouds creep closer, blocking out the scenery below. Eventually he dozes off, the sun fading to orange behind the never-ending line of clouds.

He is floating in the sky. Packs start zipping by him. Then bodies, his fellow passengers fly past him. Then the whole LGT, tumbling out of the sky. But he just floats through the air, watching the other things plummet to the earth. As they fall closer to the ground, they are consumed by dragon-like creatures that look so small from where he is. The LGT crashes to the surface, exploding into a ball of fire. He can almost feel the heat from the blast. He turns around and one of the creatures is heading straight for him. All he can see is the mouth open wide, sharp, jagged teeth lining the edges. It is about to swallow him, when it says, "Time to wake up, sleepy head."

"Time to wake up, sleepy head. Come on, get a load of this view," says 3379, jabbing him in the ribs. 3378 blinks his eyes and stretches out his arms. He turns to see out of the window. It is like they travelled into another world. The ground is a mix of orange, red, and black. The rivers run green and purple. There are no trees, but mountains and valleys line the horizon. He can see movement in the distance and other LGTs setting down on the discoloured ground. "Welcome to sector YOW."
Their LGT hits the ground and one of the supervisors stands up, "This is it, the first on your deployment mission. Use your training protocols and follow the directions of your supervisor or squad leader. Some of you will not make it back to New Europe. Know that it has been an honour to deploy with you. Those that do make it back will have seen the reason why we live like we do. Outside this door there are biochems like you have seen in the simulations, but nothing can truly prepare you for the real thing. Stay calm, use your TRM sparingly, and stay alive."

3378 was in his squad of 20, 3360-3379. 3360 was the squad leader, but most preferred 3363. If anything happened to 3360, and some secretly wished something would happen, they would vote 3363 as the new squad leader. The squad had rushed through training because of the early transition, but all of the protocols had been uploaded and each knew what to do. "Follow me. Stay close. Our objective is to get up to the mountain to provide protective fire. We got the easy job, but it is also one of the most important. If we don't succeed, our people die. Roll out!" He always said that. Apparently, it was from something people used to watch on a screen, they called it a television show. The Last Museum had a whole wing dedicated to this piece of technology that transfixed millennia of humans.

The doors to the LGT open and all he can hear are explosions and screams and the roar of something far from human.

Chapter 12

The noise starts to fade as 3378 loses his hearing. He sees 3360 motion for them to follow and he runs out of the open hatch next to his squad members. There are more explosions in the distance. Luckily, they will be further away from the heat of the action. The ground is soft, like red and orange sand. He had processed all of the information about this sector. The fifth world war caused most of the damage with the biochemical airstrikes. They tried to counter it with radiation, which killed all of the vegetation, but the strongest mutations were able to adapt and survive. So all that was left was a wasteland filled with the worst creatures imaginable.

As he steps out of the LGT, the voice of 9 echoes in his memory, "You have to get away. Something isn't right here. Don't be a hero." Seeing this other world made his head reel. What did she mean? Should he trust her? Why would he want to leave New Europe? He closes his eyes and tries to shake her voice from his mind. When he opens his eyes, he looks forward and starts to run.

They cross the flat sea of rusty earth and reach the bottom of the mountain range. 3360 calls them in, "Our targets are at the top of this hill. Create barriers close to each other and make your favourite laser sniper. Make sure all shots hit the biochems and not our own people. We hold there until they fall back." With that, he starts the charge up the 'hill'.

They reach the top and the barriers start to spring up along the ridge. 3378 moves in to look over the closest barrier. He is frozen as he surveys the battlefield below. There are tiny soldiers in groups shooting at what looks like a living version of the ancient Chinese dragons from the earlier millennia. Their bodies are long and thick, and their mouths open even wider, like they could swallow an ITM whole. Sharp fangs line their mouths, with a long thin tongue flicking out like a whip. Their heads are crowned with horns and their eyes sit just below, glowing red to match the ground. Colourful scales line their bodies, with horns down their backs and small legs near the front and back. They tunnel into the ground and pop out next to groups of attacking soldiers. For the most part, the soldiers seem to have the battle under control, but a few biochems manage to break through in the middle of a group. The unlucky ones fall into the open mouths of the biochems, their teeth shredding their bodies. 3378 can't believe what he is seeing, nor can he look away.

"Hey, get your weapon ready 78!" 3360 yells, waking him up out of his trance. He crouches behind the barrier and loads the instructions for the heavy laser sniper rifle. It starts to construct in his hands and after a few seconds, he lifts the weapon to rest on the barrier and looks down the scope. He zooms in, able to see the black slit down the middle of the eye of one creature. The soldiers below are setting barriers and spikes as the biochems get closer, trying to hold them at bay. "Fire when you have a clear shot."

3378 takes a breath in, holds his finger close to the trigger and steadies his sight on the target. His scope is filled with the eye and he squeezes his finger, sending a laser blast that tears into the head of the creature, just above the eye where he was aiming. The creature recoils back, not dead, but clearly hurt by the shot. He steadies his aim again for another shot. The rest of his squad has lined up and he notices other squads on the far ridge too. The barrage of lasers firing from above has slowed the advance of the biochems below. One falls, writhing in the sand, leaving an outline from its dying movements. The soldiers on the ground have created barriers and are using pillars to topple on the remaining creatures. 3378 wonders what all the fuss was about this threat; they had it under control in a matter of hours.

The biochems were starting to retreat, the ones still alive digging back into their holes. The field is littered with long carcasses and human bodies. Barriers had been built all over the field, their rigid gray lines contrasting with the curves of the red and orange ground. The men on the field held their lines, firing their weapons on the retreating creatures.

Just as they were almost all pushed to the back of the valley, 3378 heard a low rumble starting near the end of the mountain where they were stationed. The biochems below had stopped as the rumble began to grow louder, the ground beneath him starting to shake. Suddenly the rocks next to him explode, their constructed barriers sent flying in every direction. 3378 is knocked onto his back, for a second everything goes black. Things come back into focus, but there is a ringing in his ears.

When the dust settles, he can make out the massive shape of some gorilla-type creature with four arms, standing on two stocky legs. He has seen biochems like this in training, but never of such size. It stands at least twelve feet tall and swings its long black arms through the squad, knocking them down the slope. 3378 swings his rifle around to aim at the beast, but it is designed for long range precision, not close combat. He gets off one shot to the shoulder of the beast, but it barely slows it down. Others have composed for an attack, forming a semicircle around the creature. Some have constructed new short-range weapons and stun guns. They manage to slow its attack, but it has wiped out half of the squad. Restraints start to appear, locking its feet in place. With its last effort, it raises its four hands high into the air and slams them down on the closest soldiers. Time seems to slow as 3378 watches one hand slam down on 3360, crushing him into the ground like a jack-in-the-box being reset. Then the beast falls, shaking the earth around them.

The dragon-like creatures below begin to attack again, the massive four-armed gorillas are on the mountain ridges and 3378 sees something else pouring into the valley. They look like human-sized creatures, wearing some sort of armoured clothing. They are holding various weapons and appear to have some form of battle strategy. Watching from above, it reminds him of being in the sporting stadium. On one side of the valley, the New European soldiers are raising walls for protection. On the other side, the armoured creatures move in formation, attacking the soldiers in unison with the dragons. The gorillas have wiped out the threat from above, allowing the advance on the front below. 3378 picks up his rifle and looks down the scope. He can see what is about to happen and realizes those on the ground have no idea.

"What is it?" 3377 asks as he slides in beside 3378. He is wounded, but still able to move and fight. The close-range weapon he is holding seems in need of repair.

"We walked right into their trap. We have to get a signal to the ground." 3378 stands up, looking for where he needs to go. He sees the New European supervisors on the ground, marked with a yellow band on their arm. One looks like he is leading the charge, directing soldiers behind the battle line. "I'm going down there."

3378 creates a long thin platform, curved up at either end with little ridges in the middle. He runs and jumps on the board, propelling himself down the hill. The board skims along the surface of the mountain, cutting into the terrain and sliding over it. At first 3378 wobbles and almost loses his balance, but his protocols kick in and he bends his knees to stabilize himself. He leans into the hill to carve into the turn, slowing his speed. If it weren't for the chaos around him, he could really be enjoying this.

He is heading straight for the supervisor when a biochem dragon shoots out of the ground several feet in front of him. Digging into the sand with the edge of his board, he narrowly misses hitting the body of the creature, his hand brushing it as he glides by. As he comes out of the turn, he hits a raised part of the mountain and it sends him soaring through the air, his board slipping out from under him. He lands on his shoulders and rolls through the landing, almost making it look graceful. Luckily, he is still wearing his protective gear and the impact doesn't phase him.

Shaking off the sand, he looks around to regain his bearings. He sees the man in charge he is looking for and runs towards him, jumping over barriers and bodies. The fighting is far enough away that he doesn't worry about his safety. It only takes a minute for him to reach the supervisor. "Sir, I was up on the ridge. You have to pull your troops out. They've set a trap."

"I know," the man says as he turns to face 3378. He has a scar across his face, running through his eye. He is old and grizzled, like a pirate from the old stories. "I set it."

Chapter 13

The biochems pour out into the valley from every side. The ridges have been overrun, but the ground army is still standing behind new barriers. The horde of biochems, all different types, rush towards the wall. They outnumber the soldiers at least 5 to 1. 3378 wonders why the soldiers aren't turning and running, why the man in front of him isn't giving the order to retreat. What did he mean, he set the trap? He turns to the oncoming assault, creating a new short-range weapon. The ground beneath him rumbles with the movement from the biochems. They are feet away from the wall when the grizzled man lifts his arm above his head. "Now!"

Spikes shoot up from the ground all at once, impaling the rushing creatures, halting them dead in their tracks. Not one is left unscathed. Most have been struck fatally by several spikes, but some are still alive, squirming on the blades. The blood from the creatures starts to mix with the sand, making a rusty mud. 3378 stands in awe and horror. This was the plan all along? Why did they not know about it? Was his squad just a decoy? They lost half of their members from this trap.

"Move in slowly. Terminate anything that moves," the man yells.

3378 couldn't find his voice. He was left in shock by the sequence of events. For a second he just stood and stared as the soldiers moved between the spikes, firing on any moving corpse, and some that weren't moving. "What did you do?" The words creep out of his mouth before he realizes he spoke them.

The grizzled man slowly turns back around to face 3378. "What I did was save your sorry ass from extinction. You have 30 seconds to relocate back to your squad. If I see your face again after those 30 seconds, you will regret coming into existence." He talked with a sneer on his face, almost spitting out his words like he meant everything he said.

3378 starts running away from the slaughter. He doesn't look back, just trying to get away. His feet sink into the sand, slowing his escape. He has no idea where he is headed, he just knows he must leave. The army and the chaos shrink behind him as he runs. The valley is in the distance when he thinks of 3377 and 3379. Did they survive? Should he go back? He stops to think for a minute and remembers the words of 9 and decides to keep going.

3378's foot sinks into a hole and it sends him tumbling into the sand, his face getting covered. He gets up onto his knees and brushes the sand off his face. Just as he is able to see, the ground beneath him gives way and he is sucked under the surface. He falls several feet down the wormhole. After he lands, the sand from above falls in after him, blocking his way out. He tries to dig his way out, but the sand keeps refilling the hole. He uses his Chip to create a shovel, but nothing happens. He tries to initiate communication and still nothing. What was going on? Does the TRM not work underground? He didn't remember anything about that from his training. There were certain places where the teleportation signal could be blocked, but he didn't think solid ground would do it.

He takes a light out of his gear and shines it down the other end of the hole. It is wide enough for him to walk hunched over. The tunnel seems to continue on forever. It must come out somewhere. He starts the trek, hoping there is enough oxygen down here for him to get out.

After almost an hour of walking he comes to a fork. Which way should he go? He could end up down here forever, walking in circles. He sits and thinks for a few minutes. He decides to make a mark in one pathway and takes the other, more travelled one. He continues this for seven more forks. It seems like he has been going for hours and his light has started to fade without the solar power to regenerate it. He stops to rest his back from being hunched over.

While he lays on his back, he feels a rumble in the ground seconds before he hears it. The sound is coming from his tunnel. Without the Chip working, he has no way to protect himself. The last fork was too far back. He runs forwards, hoping a fork will appear. The sound is getting louder as he moves; he knows it is close. He scrambles forward as fast as he can, his legs barely able to hold him up. The noise is loud now, the biochem rapidly approaching. He sees the fork ahead. He is too far to tell which hole it is coming from. As he nears the fork, he can see the head of the monster down the right hole. The fork is about five feet away. With his last ounce of strength, he takes a few quick steps and dives head first to the left. The biochem brushes his feet as it travels past at full speed. He waits until it passes. Does he follow the fresh trail, or could this mean another one is on the way?

He decides to take the path more travelled again, hoping it will lead him out of this giant ant hill. After several more forks, his light finally blinks out. He fumbles his way, feeling along the walls. At the forks he feels for the one that has some warmth to it and follows that one. So, this is what it feels like to be a worm he thinks.

It takes him a few more hours of stumbling through the hole before he finally sees a light far down the tunnel. This gives him some hidden energy and he races towards it. As he comes out, he is blinded by the light after being in the dark for so long and his legs give way. He can't see, and he can't move, but he is free from the underground prison.

Slowly his vision comes back into focus and he can make out some long shapes moving in the distance, all over wherever he is. He sits up, unable to stand. After blinking, he begins to make out the shapes. He is in the hive of the biochem dragon creatures. Hundreds of them are crawling on the walls, going in and out of holes on all sides. One crawls inches away from him, seeming not to take notice of him. He rolls over and tries to stand again but falls flat on his stomach. Rolling onto his back, he sees someone standing over top of him. The person is wearing armour like the humanlike creatures from the valley. He sees a foot lift up, then feels a sharp pain, then everything goes black.

Chapter 14

When 3378 comes to, his head is pounding and his whole body is in pain. He is hanging in the middle of an empty room, his hands tied behind his back. He couldn't move, even if he wanted to. There is a faint light source in the room, but nothing else. No windows, just one door. It reminds him of the holding cell he was in before his trial. He has no idea where he is or what is happening to him. He tries again to use his Chip, but nothing happens. He feels so useless without it.

The door opens and another masked man enters holding a long staff in his right hand. He walks right up to 3378 and pokes him with the staff. "Who are you and why did you come here?" the masked man says with a gravelly voice like he is speaking through some sort of breathing apparatus. When 3378 doesn't respond, he jabs him again with the staff, harder this time. "Talk or we'll make you talk."

3378 thinks about his options and doesn't see any harm in telling this guy the truth. His history lessons mentioned some survivors outside of the wall, but it always described them as more primitive beings. What is the worst they could do to him other than kill him? "My name is 445 3378, I come from New Europe, sector L4R. I am here because I became trapped down one of the underground tunnels and I followed it to where you found me."

"Liar!" the masked man shouts and smacks 3378 across the head with his staff. Again, everything fades to black.

This time when he comes to, the room is full of people, each in some sort of mask. One beside the man with the staff walks forwards and leans in close to 3378. The mask of this one is more ornate, all in black like the others, but this one has intricate designs etched into it and pieces curving out from it as well. It is the sound of a woman's voice, "Why have you come here?" Her voice is soft and soothing. He can tell that she doesn't mean to harm him, unlike the one with the staff.

"I was just trying to get away and I fell. I had no other way to go. I'm lucky I even made it here." It is an effort to speak, his head still ringing from the last blow.

"Why did you not use your Chip to get out?" she asks, her voice hardening slightly.

"I tried, it wouldn't work." He wondered if this was giving them too much information, but he still didn't see any reason to lie. If they wanted to kill him, they would have done it by now. If they were going to torture him, then lying would only make it worse.

"Were you part of the attack?" She stands up straight as she asks this question.

"Yes, I was on the ridge. I saw the trap you had set and I ran down to warn the others. That is when I learned about the counter trap. I had nothing to do with that."

The masked woman looks to the others around her. There are murmurs amongst the crowd. He doesn't know what this means or if it made his situation better or worse. They stand looking at him for a few minutes, looking through him.

"Cut him down. Search him again, clean him, and give him new clothes. When he is ready, bring him back to me. Keep a double watch on him at all times. He doesn't seem a threat, but most real threats rarely do." With that she turns and walks out of the room. Several of the other masked people move towards him. One raises a knife and cuts the ropes suspending him in the air. He crashes to the floor.

They take him down a hall. He thinks they must be underground since there are no windows anywhere and the air feels stale. They enter another room with showers and two of the masked guards pat him down rather roughly. They tell him to take off his clothes and they push him into the shower. The water is warm, and it is the first time he feels some relief since the battle. It stings the multiple wounds he has from crawling in the tunnels and being knocked out by the guards. The dirt is ground into his skin and he can't seem to get it clean, no matter how hard he scrubs. He gives up after a while, feeling like he will have no skin left if he keeps going. They give him some fresh clothes, and, for the first time, he starts to feel normal again.

His guards walk him down another hall and to another room. This time they push him in and slam the door shut. The room is small and completely enclosed, with some long thick bars hung vertically on the walls. There is one small window where he can just barely see the guards. "Move into the middle," one says in a voice muffled by the enclosure. "It will hurt a lot less there."

What? What will hurt less? He slowly backs into the middle of the room, not knowing what is about to happen. The bars start to move out from the walls, trapping him in the centre of the room. Then they stop and he can hear a pulse coming from the bars. A severe pain whips through his body, like a million hornets all stinging him at once. It is a pain so strong that he wishes he could die in that instant, so it would be over, but it lasts for about ten seconds. The bars stop pulsing and retract back into the walls. 3378 collapses on the floor, thankful it is over, but still wishing he was dead.

Chapter 15

The ball comes flying at 3378's head. He narrowly dodges it and sends up a wall flinging it back towards 9. A wall pops up right in front of 9 as the ball approaches and ricochets off the brick and flies back towards 3378.

"Come on 8, you can do better than that!" 9 yells, taunting her opponent.

Three barriers pop up in succession on 3378's side of the playing field and the ball pinballs off the walls, building speed with each collision. Flying at triple speed, the ball aims for 9 again. This time she dives, the ball barely missing her back. A wall appears near the back of the playing field, sending the ball to the far right.

"Ha! I got you this time!" 3378 gloats as the ball drifts far off target.

9 slowly gets to her feet. A wall redirects the path of the ball to the other side of the field, then another one redirects it again, then another and another. 3378 tries to keep track of the ball but loses it in the myriad of walls. He looks both left and right, trying to locate the ball, but all he sees are walls. The sound of the ball bouncing off the walls lets him know that it is near max speed. He starts to retreat to the back of his side when one of the walls shatters and the ball shoots out at lighting speed. 3378 looks over his shoulder just in time to see the ball as it smashes into his back, sending him flying to the ground.

"Who got who?" 9 asks as she stands over 3378.

"Ya ya ya. You win, yet again." 3378 winces as 9 helps him to his feet. The ball doesn't break bones, but it leaves a solid bruise when it hits at full speed.

The field blinks as the simulation shuts down and they step out of the simulator.

"Why do you always make yourself taller in the simulation?" 9 asks.

"I need every advantage I can get," he replies, not making eye contact.

"Size isn't measured in feet and inches, it's measured in the kindness of the soul. That's where humanity went wrong, we started measuring the wrong things. We lost sight of what really mattered."

"That escalated quickly."

"You know what I mean. We put too much importance on appearances instead of what things are really like."

"Ya, I guess."

"It's useless trying to talk to you!"

3378 wakes up in a bed, more comfortable than his own that he had slept in for the last 15 years. He shakes his head thinking about the dream that was more like a memory than anything else. The room is still underground, but the air feels fresher and there is a slight breeze, making it feel like it is beside the ocean. His pain from earlier is gone and the paralyzing shock seems like a distant memory, like a dream that felt so real. He sits up in his bed and sees a plate of food and a drink on the table beside him. He devours it in seconds. He is so hungry he doesn't even consider if it is safe to eat or not. He eats so fast that he feels sick and looks for a place in case he has to throw up.

As he is stumbling around the room, the door opens, and a woman comes in. She is not wearing a mask and she is unlike any woman from New Europe. Her hair is a golden blond and she is tall and slender, but very muscular too. Her skin is more pale than anyone he has ever seen. The breeze catches her hair and blows it back. Her face is stunningly beautiful, but she appears to be missing one eye. 3378 blinks, thinking his mind is playing tricks on him and he has finally lost it.

"If you're wondering if what you are seeing is correct, it is. I was born with one eye, which is why I am here. I assume your lessons did not teach you about us, so I am here to inform you. If you want to leave at any time, you can. I am sorry for the pain of the De-tech room, but it was necessary to make sure you were telling the truth and your Chip was not active. The room disables TRMs. We have had several of your people try to infiltrate us and take us out from the inside. Some were more successful than others, but we have become fairly proficient in our sorting process." She spoke in an even tone.

"Who are you? Where am I? What is this place?" He had too many questions to ask, so much he wanted to know.

"It will take a while to explain everything. It is best that I show you to better understand. I am Eliza, one of those in charge of this place. This place is The Last Refuge, in what you would call sector U7N. It is what used to be known as Asia or Mongolia to be more specific. We are thirty feet underground. Any aboveground buildings we had were destroyed by the New Europe armies." She gave him a slight glare with the last statement.

"Armies? We don't have armies. Everyone goes through deployment to stop the threat of the biochems."

"And what did your lessons tell you about us humans?"

"That there were few of you and you were mostly primitive beings." Things were starting to click in 3378's head.

"Like I said, you need to see some things for yourself."

They travel through several corridors and end up at some sort of underground transit system. There is a long tube running from either end of the corridor. A hatch on the side opens. Eliza motions for 3378 to enter, but he can't quite tell how he is supposed to get in. "Just hop in and lie down. Try not to move too much. Close the hatch when you get out." He swings one leg in and then the other and crouches into the tube, lying on his back. Eliza closes the hatch and presses some buttons. He is shot through the tube like an air powered waterslide from the 21st century. There are several turns, drops, and inclines. It might actually be enjoyable if he knew that he wasn't about to die. After about a minute, he comes to a slow stop and another hatch opens. He gets out and closes the hatch. Eliza arrives a minute later.

They climb a tall ladder that leads to an opening above ground. The light is blinding, like someone is shining a spotlight in his eyes. The white light starts to fade and he sees that he is surrounded by lush greenery. Tall colourful trees and vegetation cover the ground and area. It is the most beautiful view he has ever seen. He follows Eliza through the trees, marveling at the sights. Why was there so much about the world that was left out of his lessons? Why was this woman treating him like this? Why wasn't he locked away in some dungeon?

They come up to a concrete building which seemed oddly out of place in this vast woodland area. There are no windows or openings in the building except for an entrance-way in the middle. "You will be able to get in since you are from New Europe. When you enter, tell them your number and say that you are there to inspect the premises. There are just automatons in there, so don't be afraid. I will be waiting outside when you come out. Don't do or touch anything, just observe."

3378 walks over to the entrance and stands in front of it for a few seconds. A red light flashes and beeps and the doors open. He walks in and feels the cold air wash over him like an arctic wave. Inside he is greeted by an automaton. "Hello, welcome to the sector U7N processing facility. I am AF27789. Please state your name and purpose of visit." She is overly friendly but looks just like anyone else from New Europe. It gives him an eerie sense of home, something he had not thought about for some time.

"445 3360. I am here to inspect the premises." He thought it best to use the old squad leader's name, in case his number had been reported as missing. He hoped the death register had not been processed yet. It usually took several days from deployment for it to go through. Thinking about that, he realized he didn't know what day it was. Too late now.

"Welcome 445 3360. We did not expect an inspection for another 15.3 days. Under whose orders are you here for inspection?" Still the friendly tone, but it was clearly unfitting now.

"421 3347," he says the first reasonable thing that comes to his mind. Hopefully that doesn't get either of them into trouble. "This is a surprise inspection because of all the activity in the area." He can feel himself digging deeper and deeper.

"Very well, please begin your inspection. Thank you for your visit." Her smile stays glued to her face as she watches him walk by.

As he moves inside the facility, a million questions start forming in his brain. What the heck is this place? Why is it so secretive? What did Eliza want him to see? Who was she anyway? The inside of the building opens up to a massive room with rows and rows of people. He is on a balcony above and looks down to survey the room. Each person is working on something in front of them. There must be thousands of people in here, all focused intently on the item in front of them. A few people holding guns walk slowly between the rows. There is no talking, just the sound of the work being done. He takes the stairway to the ground floor to get a closer look.

Each row is filled with people sitting at a table, huddled over something in front of them. Most of them have the New European look, but a few are very different. Some have the pale skin like Eliza, some are missing a limb, some have red eyes. No one looks away from their task.

Slowly, he walks between the rows, trying to figure out what is happening here. As he reaches the first row, he sees a man, slightly older than him, probably year 35. He is hunched over a scrap of an ITM, using some sort of tool to trace it. As he traces it, each piece the tool touches disappears. He is so intent on what he is doing that he doesn't even flinch as 3378 walks by.

The next person is a woman, much older. She is tracing a gun, similar to the one he was using in the battle. The next is a young boy working on a piece of clothing. Each person is doing the same thing, deconstructing some discarded creation. 3378 thinks back to his year of debris collection. All the waste they teleported ended up at a place like this to be refined and sent back to New Europe. He starts to realize why he is here. This is how New Europe is possible, but who are these people? Why are they so focused on their work? Then, seven people down the row, he recognizes someone.

Sitting in front of a cement barrier, calmly tracing each little section, is the girl from the crash. He quickly walks towards her, forgetting where he is and what he is doing. He stops in front of her station and she doesn't look up. "Hey, what are you doing here?" he asks in a quiet, rushed voice. Again, she doesn't look up. He grabs her free arm and shakes it. "Can't you hear me?" This is a little louder and it travels, being the only voice in the whole place.

One of the patrol guards stops his route to turn towards where 3378 is. The girl looks up at 3378, her eyes empty. She seems like she is about to say something, but nothing comes out. The guard starts walking towards him. "We have to get out of here. Now!" He starts pulling on her arm, but she doesn't move. He falls down, trying to move her again. The guard gets to his row and is coming quickly towards him. He looks over at the girl and sees she is strapped into her seat.

"Hey, what are you doing?" the guard demands, raising his weapon and moving closer to where 3378 is on the floor. 3378 scrambles up and starts to back away.

"I am here for the inspection. This unit was not responding." He tries to bluff his way out again.

"What is your name?" the guard asks and stops, holding his weapon straight at 3378's head.

"445 3360. I am here for the inspection." 3378 keeps backing down the row, his hands in front of him.

"Stop where you are. Your number is not able to process. You will have to report to the facility director immediately." The guard readies his weapon. 3378 can tell it is one that shoots a stunning bolt. One shot from that and he will be knocked out cold. He can't risk going to the director, they will know he is lying when they scan him. Was this part of Eliza's plan?

He has backed up to the old woman. He reaches down at her table and grabs the gun and fires it as soon as it is pointed in the guard's direction. The barrel had been deconstructed so the laser blasts in several directions, knocking the guard back and hitting several other workstations. He hesitates for a second, looking at the damage he caused. He moves to unstrap the girl, but the guard sits up and shoots at him, just missing his shoulder. Grabbing the gun again, 3378 hops over the table and runs towards the entrance where he came in. He can hear the guard calling for backup, but he doesn't waste time looking back. The stairs don't slow him down as he takes them two at a time.

At the top he is greeted by AF27789, blocking his way and still smiling. "Please report to the-" He knocks her in the face, but it barely phases her. "You shouldn't do that." She grabs his wrist and twists it, forcing him to his knees. He pulls his gun up and shoots over his chest in the automaton's direction. It hits her in the chest, arm and leg, sending her into the wall and freeing him. He stands up and runs to the door. He can hear the guards climbing the stairs. The door won't open. He tries to blast it with the laser, but nothing happens. The guards must have set the alarm and locked him in. He turns around with his half-deconstructed gun, ready to face the assault. The footsteps of the guards reach the top of the stairs. He puts his finger on the trigger, ready to unleash whatever would come out of this gun. Just as the first guard turns the corner, he hears the door behind him slide open. He doesn't even have time to see what happened when he is yanked through the doorway.

Chapter 16

The air flows by 3378 as he is lifted into the air. Someone had grabbed him from behind as the guards turned the corner and opened fire on him. He was pulled into the air by a 21st century vehicle with air propelling blades. They sail over the facility, his body dangling in the air, held by his unknown rescuer. The forest looks just as majestic from above, the concrete building even more out of place. They set down in an open field a few miles away. He is let go and drops to the ground. "What happened in there?" he hears Eliza's voice ask.

"I saw someone I knew. I was trying to get her out. What was going on in there? What happened to those people?"

"Some are there because they broke your laws. Some didn't fit the genetic norms of your society. Now they make sure that you can use your Chips to make anything you want." He could taste the contempt in her voice.

"I didn't do any of this. I had no idea any of this was going on."

"None of you ever do. It's not your fault. It just makes me so furious. The Chip doesn't just go one way. That's how they control the people in there. That's why we had to zap you when you came in. It is how New Europe is able to function. There are hundreds of those facilities over the planet, breaking down materials to the base matter that can teleport and blend to create new materials. New Europe depends on a fine balance and if anything upsets that balance, it all falls apart.

"If they have too many people, the resources would run out. If they run out of resources, the Chip won't function. Too few people and the work doesn't get done. The members are just weights in the balance. Move one to the other side to keep it all in check."

"How do you know all this?"

"Because I used to be a member. Come, there is someone else you need to see."

They travel in the air propelled vehicle several miles to the south. It was much better riding inside than hanging from below.

They set down in a clearing and head towards another underground hatch.

As they open the hatch, Eliza grabs 3378's shoulder. "Before you go in, I should warn you. What you will hear is the truth, even if you don't want to believe it. Keep your mind open and you will learn all you need to know." The look in her eye was serious and full of concern, like she didn't want him to slip away.

They climb down the ladder, into a bunker similar to the first one he entered. They pass several rooms, not seeing any people until they come to a large room at the end of the hallway. The room looks like some sort of ramshackle medical centre. Sitting in the middle of the room is an old man with white hair and lines carved in his skin. His features are old, but he moves with the ability of youth as he jumps up to greet Eliza. They embrace and he turns to look at 3378, scanning him up and down.

"What have you brought me Eliza?" the old man asks.

"Alex, this is 445 3378. He came through the worm tunnels. We just came from the deconstruction facility. We had a close call as he decided to try a rescue mission." She is joking, but still talking in a serious tone.

"I see. What did the scan show?"

"Sympathetic. Curious, but also wary."

"And you felt him ready?" he asks with a sideways glance towards her.

"Ready as any of them. We are running out of time. We can't keep-"

"Don't talk to me of time," he snaps at Eliza. He turns to 3378, "Come with me. We have much to discuss." He leads 3378 into another room, almost like a dental office with one of the large chairs in the middle.

"So, what would you like to know?" he asks, sitting back in a comfortable chair in a corner of the room. The question catches him off guard. There is so much he wants to know that he doesn't know where to start.

"Who are you and why are you helping me?" He asks the thing most pressing to him at the moment.

"My name is Alex. Like Eliza, I was once a member of New Europe. I escaped about 30 years ago. I was on my own in the beginning, but I soon met some of the native inhabitants. Like you, I had no idea they existed. They took me as a prisoner, but eventually saw that I was not a threat to them and took me in as one of their own. It had been a few centuries since the formation of New Europe, so their language had evolved quite a bit from our English and their social customs had devolved to something more tribal. With their help, I freed a few more New Europeans over the years and we found some underground bases from the last world war that we were able to use for our purposes.

"I am helping you for the same reason I helped free all the others. The wall wasn't built to keep people out, it was built to keep you in and shelter you from the real world outside. Why do you think you don't really know anything about the world outside? You know exactly what they want you to know and you think exactly what they want you to think. Since you have seen the facility, you know some of the truth.

"What do you think was going to happen to your trial when you returned? Do you really think you would be set free after a valiant effort on the battlefield? New Europe has one purpose: keep New Europe functioning, at any cost. The members are just a tool to keep things running; each one is expendable." The old man knew that was a lot to process, so he took a breath and sat back for a second.

3378's brain was hurting. "What happens to the people in the deconstruction facilities?"

"They work each day, processing the waste of New Europe so it can be used again. They eat and sleep like a human, but they don't function like one. They are controlled through the Chip, so there is no pain in their monotony, but they are essentially dead. They don't live as long as normal-"

"Why don't they just use automatons?"

"The materials used to make an automaton are too scarce to make the numbers needed. Humans are created at virtually no cost."

"What is it that you want from me? Why go through all this trouble for one person?"

"To us, each person is worth the effort. We can't free all of New Europe, but we can save a few each year. And with your help, we might be able to do more."

"What do you mean?"

"Most of the people we save are from the facilities or have been hurt in fighting. You are one of the few that made it to us with no damage to your Chip. They disconnected you when you went off the grid, but we can hook you back up."

"What? How?"

"We have the ability to hack into your Chip and unlock all of the doors. It would give you full access to the whole database of protocols and info resources. It would be the Chip like you know it, but with no limitations."

"What's the catch?" This was sounding too good to be true. He had felt cut off from the world as soon as his Chip stopped working. Why would they disconnect him? Did they think him dead?

"If we help you, you would help us. You are the only one able to get back into New Europe. We would ask you to help us free the world by breaking into the New Europe archives to steal the Chip plans for us. They are stored on one Intel Chip that is in the heart of New Europe. This would create an equal playing field for all those outside of the walls of New Europe. We wouldn't have to live underground anymore. We could free all those imprisoned in the facilities. And you would be their saviour."

If he thought his head hurt before, now it was about to explode. He was being offered ultimate power, but only if he agreed to destroy everything he had ever known. "What is the other option?"

"We can take the Chip out and you live like the rest of us, hiding underground, fighting an unstoppable army."

"Can't I just walk away?"

"Sure, you could. Where would you go? How would you survive? If the biochems didn't get you, the patrols would and you would end up with your friend working on the facility line. Look, I know this is a lot to take in. You don't need to decide right now, but we are running out of time. Sleep on it and let us know tomorrow. If you need anything, Eliza will help you." He gestures that he could leave and he turns in his chair and picks up a book, suggesting that he was done answering questions. 3378 stands up, his head reeling, and walks out the door.

Chapter 17

A long, dark corridor looms ahead of 3378. In the distance he can hear screams of pain. He starts running to the sound. He turns a corner and enters a large room. All around there are people tied up, hanging from the ceiling. In the middle of the room is a woman on a chair. The screams are coming from her as someone stands over her. 3378 tries to yell, but nothing comes out. He moves closer and is able to make out the face of the woman. It is 445 0009. The person over her is dressed in medical gear with a surgical mask over their face. The person is about to cut into 9 with a knife when 3378 reaches out and grabs the arm holding the knife. The surgeon reaches up and pulls off the mask, revealing the face of 455 7042, a blank stare meeting 3378's eyes.

3378 looks down and sees blood all over 9. He looks to his hands and they are covered in blood and he is holding the knife. He looks around and the room is covered in blood. 42 moves towards him and puts her hands around his neck to choke him. He tries to scream, but nothing comes out.

He wakes up screaming. He is soaked in sweat and his hands are stained red with blood. He opens his fists to see cuts caused by his fingernails being dug into his palms. It is still dark in the room. The stale underground air blankets him, the only sound his heavy breathing. Alone in the dark, he stands to make sure he is not still in a dream. He runs the water in the sink and rinses the blood from his hands, the water in the sink turning a light red as it dilutes the blood. He throws some of the water in his face and looks into the mirror. The face looking back at him is not one he recognizes. His eyes are sunk, his skin dark and rugged. What was happening to him?

Lying back down, he is restless and unable to fall back to sleep or afraid to. After hours of staring at the ceiling, tossing and turning, he gives up and walks around the room. It is an impossible decision he has to make. Does he accept the ultimate power and destroy everything he has ever known or does he relinquish it forever and fade away. There was no right decision and no easy answer.

A light reflected through mirrors shines into the room, signaling the first rays of the dawn and the sands of time running out. Eliza walks into the room, "Time to get up and moving. We have something for you to eat." She brings in a plate filled with food, nothing like the food from New Europe. There were things on there that he had never seen before. Such rich colours and textures that it almost made him sick. As it was, he didn't think he could eat anything anyway.

After picking at an orange leafy thing, he decided he just wanted to get on with everything. "Can we see Alex now?"

"Soon. Have you made a decision?"

"Yes. At least I think I have." He had gone back and forth a million times through the night and thought about running more than once. It came down to which decision could he live with. While he wasn't 100%, he was close enough.

This time they travelled by the tubes all the way to the medical centre. When they got there, it was bustling with people, the complete opposite of the last time he was there. Nobody seemed to be under duress, but there was a seriousness to each person they passed.

They arrive at Alex's office and it looks like it is set up for surgery. Eliza stops and looks at 3378, "This is where I leave you. I'll be back when it's all over. I trust you will make the right decision." She gives him a long look which says much more than her words before she turns and walks away.

Alex stands up as 3378 enters the room and moves to greet him, "Welcome back. I trust you had a good sleep and large breakfast." The sarcasm was not lost on him, nor was it appreciated. "What's it going to be? Chip or no Chip?"

"Before I tell you my decision, I have a few items to discuss." This had been part of what he worked out in his head last night. If he was going to play their game, he was damn sure he would get something out of it for himself.

"Very well. Let's hear them." Alex crosses his arms.

"Whatever I choose, you free 455 7042 from the facility."

"Woah, it isn't that simple. You saw how tight the security is in those places."

"Also, you will get a message from me to 445 0009. Letting her know the truth and what happened to me."

"Hold on. We can't just broadcast our presence. I don't think you understand how things work here."

"No, you don't understand how things work!" He wasn't sure what he meant by that, but it sounded good in his head. "If I am going to trust you and put my life in your hands, you have to give me something. No matter what, people are going to die. I just want to try to save a few. I know you need me, otherwise you wouldn't have gone through all this trouble. I also know you are running out of time and resources. The New European armies are trying to wipe you out. Each day they move closer and closer. I don't want to destroy New Europe, but I want to help make things right."

"So you are going to help us?"

"Can you guarantee my demands?"

"I can promise that we will do everything we can to try."

"No, do or do not. There is no try!" he yells. He had heard that somewhere before and thought it appropriate to use now.

"Okay, okay. We'll do it. Even better, you will do it," Alex says with a slight grin on his face.

"Good. Let's get this over with."

Alex motions for 3378 to sit in the chair. They strap his arms down and his legs and head. "This is going to hurt a bit. We have to cut in to hook up to the Chip. Unfortunately, freezing could damage the circuits, so we can't risk it."

"Talking about it isn't making it any better. Just get on with it already." 3378 grips the handles of the chair. Alex grabs a knife from the table beside the chair.

The blade inches closer to his neck, but he isn't sure if this is what he wants anymore. Was he willing to give up everything that he'd ever known? He can feel the blade begin to pierce his skin. In a moment of hesitation, he cries out for it to stop. Is this the right decision? He needs an answer. Why is he here? How did he get here? What would happen next? Was everything all a lie? He takes a deep breath. This decision could affect all of humanity. He knows what he needs to do, but he isn't sure if he is strong enough to do it.

The blade stops, just pricking the back of his neck. "Keep going," he says and the blade jabs through his skin.

The pain is excruciating, like a burning needle being sawed into the back of his neck. He jerks in the chair, held down by the restraints. He screams out for some sort of release. As the blade slides deeper into his neck, he can feel his heart pounding through his chest. The restraints holding him down start to cut into his skin as he pushes against them as hard as he can. He starts to wish he had made a different decision, that he could be rid of all of this forever. Everyone he ever cared about no longer seems worth the pain he is enduring right now.

"There. We're in," Alex says, like he just landed an ITM. "It will take a while to hack in and upload the data. Sit back and relax, the worst of it is over."

He could still feel the pain in his memory, his whole body numb from the shock. As he starts to regain feeling, it is like a wave of pain crashes over him all at once. After a few seconds he passes out.

When he wakes he sees Alex sitting by a screen, watching numbers constantly change. He doesn't know how long he was out, but gets the sense that this will not be quick. While he waits, he thinks about what might happen. The most likely outcome to each scenario is that he dies. The next is that he rescues some people and dies. Perhaps he makes it back to New Europe and actually gets inside and steals the Intel Chip, what then? There are too many different possible endings that it starts to add to the pain in his neck. The whole ordeal overwhelms him, and he passes out in the chair.

Chapter 18

There is a clicking sound in the room from a fan hanging loosely from the ceiling. 3378's eyes open at the sound and he stares at the spinning fan for several minutes, not knowing where he is. The last thing he remembers is the pain, the pain of a thousand stab wounds to his neck. He sits up slowly, his whole body feeling the pain now. Eliza is at the door to his room, a ramshackle recovery room. "How do you feel?" she asks, leaning in the doorway.

"Like I got run over by an LGT." He can barely open his eyes.

"It should get better in a day or two. Come on, we need to test it out."

"No time to relax, eh?" His mind is still racing. What had he done? Was this the right decision? What would happen next? His tired mind could not keep up with the myriad of questions that raced through his head.

"We have less time than we thought. The armies are closing in as we speak. It was a small miracle that we found you when we did."

"Ya, I don't know if I feel the same. I'm like a human guinea pig."

"Well, you're not the first to have the modification done."

"No? What happened to the others?" Why didn't he ask this before? Was he right to put his faith in these people? Still too many questions and not enough answers.

"That's a story for another time," Eliza says stoically.

"I guess it's one I don't want to hear." He pulls on his shirt and pants as he slides out of his bed. Eliza leads him down the hall and through a tube to the surface. From the exit they walk for a few minutes until they reach a clearing. She motions for him to follow and he steps out into the sunshine. It is blinding like the last time he was below ground for a period of time. How could anyone get used to living underground?

"Okay, so you have a whole new set of protocols and information access to work with. Today we will test some out to make sure your Chip is going to work. Over the next few days we will train you on some of the others, whatever we have time for.

"The New European armies are moving closer to our base. They must have gained access to our coordinates. I guess a few people survived that massacre that you witnessed. For years New Europe has been trying to weed us out. We were able to hide at first, then we started to fight back. Lately we have been losing the battle though." She spoke solemnly, not accusing him this time. She is quiet for a time as they walk through the trees and into a clearing.

"The first test is the elevating wall. You can make standard walls all you want, but the elevating wall can shoot someone into the air. It was banned because it was causing too many serious injuries and even a few deaths. It was particularly dangerous when used in the sporting events. Load the protocol for elevating wall and try it out in the field."

3378 uses his Chip to access the protocol. It is strangely comforting to have his Chip active again, like coming home after a few hours in the simulators. He looks out into the field and tells the Chip to make the wall. A wall shoots up and back down so fast that he almost missed it. "That wasn't what I meant to do."

"This is like having a new Chip. It is like you are a baby learning how to use it from the beginning. You know the basics, but most things are going to work a bit differently. Try it again," Eliza says in a soothing voice, like a patient teacher.

This time he concentrates, and three walls shoot up from the ground, launching a layer of earth 30 feet into the air. "Okay, I got this," he says as he prepares to go again. This time a solid wall shoots up from the ground and stays there. "Yes!"

"Good. We just have another twenty thousand to go through. Don't worry, it will get easier. Try the mechanical dog." He knew what dogs were from the videos in the Last Museum, but he had never seen one in real life.

They go through about thirty more protocols before they quit. Some are more successful than others, but 3378 is physically and mentally exhausted by the end. He doesn't know how long he can keep going at this pace. "Okay, get some rest and we will come back tomorrow. You did well today. Not a master student, but not the worst we've had."

"Wait. Why do you need the Intel Chip so bad? What will it actually change?" He needed at least some answers to go on.

"Having the Intel Chip will change everything. It will allow us to recreate Chips for everyone. We won't have to hide and run from New Europe anymore. We can free all those trapped in the facilities." A glow appears in her pale skin as she talks.

"But won't New Europe fight back? They won't just let you do all this without retribution."

"That's what we are hoping for." Her lips curl and there is something in her eyes that shows her true emotion.

As soon as 3378 gets back, he lies down and blacks out. Eliza is there again the next morning, just like the last. They keep repeating the training, adding larger numbers of protocols each day as he becomes more proficient at learning new ones. Some are fairly dangerous, so Eliza sets up safety precautions which slows things down, but 3378 is glad she does. One explosive protocol goes off sideways and hits the invisible barrier right in front of Eliza. It would have taken her head off otherwise.

On the fifth day, 3378 is starting to feel normal again and has gotten used to the pace and demand of the training. He jumps out of bed just as Eliza arrives and is eager to get to work. "Let's go. What are we going through today? Mechanical shark cannons?" She doesn't laugh, making him look a little embarrassed by his joke.

"Change of plans. Your training is being cut short. The armies have hit our exterior outposts. We are heading to New Europe tonight. Everyone here is either evacuating or setting up a defensive stand."

"Wait. What? I've only learned a few hundred of the protocols. I'm not even good at most of them. What about 42? Alex promised we would free her." He was frantic with the thought of having to go through with everything right now and them trying to go back on their deal.

"Yes, we know. We have a plan to get her today. It is not ideal, but it is the best we have with no time. Grab your stuff, we head out in an hour."

3378 grabs the few things he has acquired during his stay. He doesn't know what to think, but luckily doesn't have much time to do so. Eliza is back down in exactly an hour, a pack on her back and belt equipped with different weapons.

"So, what's the plan?" 3378 asks, none of the earlier excitement in his voice.

***

They arrive at the facility by air again, but this time it looks like a giant tomb in the middle of a multicoloured graveyard garden. Eliza had briefed him of the plan on the ride, and it was the most preposterous thing he had ever heard. Not only did it involve him using protocols he had never practiced, it required precision timing without any sort of rehearsal. He seriously considered revoking his request to save 42 when he heard the plan.

The vehicle sets down just outside of the facility grounds. They have exactly five minutes to execute their plan and evacuate the premises before support arrives. "You ready?" Eliza asks.

"No."

"Not the best answer, but it's too late to go back now. Start each step at the signal. We get one shot at this and if you mess it up, we all die."

"That's reassuring."

They run out of the vehicle and spread in different directions. 3378 is at a distance directly lined up with the corner of the facility. He has the most important role and they can't afford having anything happen to him. Eliza is within shouting distance, but they had gone through the hand signals, just in case.

She motions for him to start the first step. He starts building a shape on top of the facility. In the center is a circular shell, like that of a beetle. Slowly, pieces start to attach to the shell and two spindly legs stretch over each side of the building when it is done. It looks like a giant spider is spread over the whole facility.

Eliza motions again. 3378 starts the second step and long jagged metal blades appear the width of each wall near the base. In unison, they start sawing back and forth, cutting into the foundation. In a few seconds, they have pierced the outer walls.

A third motion sees the spider attach to the facility and lift it straight up off the foundation. The legs of the spider extend, and the building walls are raised into the air and then lifted to the side, exposing the whole inside of the facility. There is a second of shock as this happens by all those inside as they are paralyzed momentarily. Eliza and the others seize the brief opportunity and converge on the opened facility. They neutralize the guards before they can fire back. The rest of the people sitting at the workstations continue to plod away at their task, oblivious that their encasement has been ripped open.

Eliza gets to 42 first, cuts the restraints holding her in and yanks her out of her chair. She reaches for her deconstructing tool as she is carried by the waist out of the open building. As they emerge from the building, a guard fires from a half standing position, hitting Eliza in the leg. She falls, sending 42 forward to the ground. When 42 gets up, she starts running back to the building. Eliza grabs her leg, tripping her. "A little help here!" she yells to 3378, who is watching with a stunned look on his face. He puts up a barricade between 42 and the building, trapping her with Eliza. The guard, now on his feet, takes aim at one of their people. Just as he fires, a spider leg comes crashing down on his head. His shot misses and the crew make their way back to the vehicle, both Eliza and 42 being carried.

"Restrain her in the back, she will leap out if given the chance," Eliza commands.

"You're hurt. Is it bad?" 3378 asks, not really wanting the truth. They set Eliza down in the vehicle and he gets a good look at the wound. There is a large tear down the back of her lower leg, with blue ooze glistening at either end of the opening. He can see her tibia and knows the damage is severe.

　　"Load your information bank on cold fire wounds. See if you can get me back to the base." With that her eyes close. The vehicle lifts into the air.

　　3378 loads all the information banks he can find. Most of what he gets is not good news, extensive nerve damage, complete muscle loss, death from blood poisoning. After a minute of downloading, he knows the only course of action, as terrible as it may be. "Strap her down any way you can," he orders the others. A strap appears around her thigh and he pulls it tight. He gets the protocol for an automated medical saw and creates one in his hands. "Hold her tight and look away." He brings the saw just below her knee, above the top of the wound and starts the blade spinning. He presses down and the blood splatters everywhere, covering those holding her down. In seconds it cuts through the bone and flesh to the other side. A bandage starts to wrap around her leg, holding the blood in the wound. It is enough to get her back to the base.

Chapter 19

They rush Eliza to the medical center at the base when they land. 3378 is left to take care of 42. She is almost in worse shape than Eliza. Her mouth is foaming and her head keeps twitching. Her eyes are open, but she is not looking at anything specific. The info on facility rehabilitation is slim, but he learns that she needs her Chip reset and a few days of rest. She won't be the same as before, but she will be able to function like a human again. Luckily, she was not in the facility very long. The longer in there, the less chance there is for recovery.

The medical centre is overrun with casualties. The fighting on the perimeter must have started already. 3378 finds a free nurse that is willing to take 42, but he doesn't seem happy about it. Everyone is running around frantically, people are screaming, blood coats the floor and walls. 3378 looks around, scanning for Eliza. He sees her in an operating chair, they are already unwrapping her bandage. Her eye is slowly blinking open and closed. As he moves next to her, she moves her head as if she recognizes him. With a laboured breath, she speaks, "You have to finish the mission. It is now or never. Alex has uploaded everything you need to know. I believe in -" Before her last word she goes unconscious again. 3378 grabs her hand and squeezes it, partly for her, and partly to keep himself from losing it completely. He doesn't know if he can do this alone. He doesn't know what will happen. All he knows is that he has to try.

He runs out of the base and climbs through the hatch. He can hear the fighting in the distance, it isn't close, but it is still loud. As he moves, he accesses the upload from Alex. It is Alex's voice that he hears, "It appears that everything we have built and worked for has been compromised. Now, you are our last hope. In a few days, we will be overrun by the New Europe armies. If any of us survive, we will relocate to sector M4N. All of our resources and equipment will be destroyed. Our only chance at surviving is if you can get the Intel Chip. The Intel Chip contains everything we need to reproduce Chips for those outside of New Europe. With

Chips, we can stand up to New Europe and start to build a place to live again.

"For years we have been trying to find someone with an active Chip that is willing to fight for our cause and make things right in the world. You did not come to us by chance. Thank you for giving us a reason to believe."

Woah, that is a lot to put on one person, 3378 thinks. He accesses the rest of the plan details and sees how it could work, in theory. An ITM begins to construct in front of him. He keeps wondering how he got here, why him? What happens if he doesn't succeed? The ITM opens and he steps in. It lifts off and heads towards New Europe. He thought ITMs couldn't function outside of New Europe...

After a long, but uneventful journey, 3378 sees the giant walls of New Europe on the horizon. His feeling of home is mixed with his newfound contempt for everything that New Europe now embodied. He replayed the instructions many times during the trip so that he had them memorized without accessing his Chip. He knew that he did not have any time to waste as those he left behind had their backs against the wall.

Once 3378 gets within eyesight of the wall he sets his ITM down in the trees. If he is spotted before he gets over the wall, it would be over and he would likely end up in a facility or dead. Following the plan, he heads to the southeast section. There he finds the water refuse tunnel. He constructs a saw and cuts through the bars. Holding his breath, he jumps into the murky water and swims against the stream. The long journey makes his muscles seize as he kicks through the current. He doesn't have far to go, but he is running out of air. With a final push of his whole body, he makes it to the opening inside. There is a small hole used to check the water for blockages and he is just able to squeeze through. Had he been any larger, this plan would not have worked already.

Inside the city, he creates a set of standard New European clothes and changes out of his wet ones. Not much he could do about the smell though. The plan directs him to the administration complex, a place he had only been to a handful of times in his life.

With the site plan, he knew exactly where to go and who he needed to avoid. The modified Chip also granted him access to any doors that would normally be locked to him. This was almost way too easy; a little kid could follow this plan with ease. He locates the main holding room and heads to the case that would hold the Intel Chip he was looking for. Just grab it and retrace his steps and it was done. Simple. Except the Intel Chip isn't where it is supposed to be!

3378 looks up and sees 421 3347 standing in front of him. He is holding the Intel Chip in his hands. "Is this what you are looking for?" He holds it out for 3378 to see.

"It doesn't have to be like this. There is more to this world than what you have behind these walls." 3378 is sad to see his old supervisor, the one who helped him through many difficult years. This was the one person that could get to him, but New Europe knew that, that was why he was here. But how did they know he would be coming?

"Do you know what the world was like before New Europe? Before we lived behind these walls? The world was overrun with humans, people were starving and dying everywhere. People would kill other people in the streets for food or money. A few owned all the wealth and hoarded it for themselves while everyone else fought for the scraps like stray dogs. Money brought out the greed and envy of humanity. The waste was killing the planet. Garbage, debris, emissions were rapidly killing life of all forms. Before World War 4, the planet was days away from complete destruction. The war wiping out half of humanity was the best thing possible. From this, the intellects of the world realized that the only way to survive was through strict population control. Once the Chip was created, we were able to eliminate all types of production. It took over 300 years after World War 5 to perfect the equations and numbers, but we finally found the perfect equilibrium."

"At the expense of those that didn't fit your vision of perfection." He tried to think of 3347 as part of New Europe, part of the horror he had seen.

"It was the price we were willing to pay to save humanity. Everyone who started New Europe agreed that this was a sacrifice we were willing to make to protect life from the corruption and chaos that was the past."

"No one else agreed to it though! You just kept it hidden from everyone and lied about what was really happening."

"You think people want to know the truth? Go out there and tell them what you saw, tell them all you know. People have tried before. You know what happened? Nothing. People continue on in their lives and comfort. All reality is constructed and we have made the best possible reality we can. One that can last for millennia. You give the Chip to those vagabonds and you will destroy everything that has been built to save humanity, to save this planet, to save life. We go back to trading and hoarding. We go back to fighting and killing. We go back to destruction and chaos."

"But what is life without freedom?"

"Don't you get it? With freedom, there is no life. Our way is the only way to survive." His anger was starting to rise.

"But you control people through the Chip."

"Is that what they told you? Then why weren't you controlled? We don't control people, it is more of a guidance. When people are left to their own impulses, the result is pain and suffering. If the Chip can help prevent that, who would not want that? People aren't fully controlled except for in the facilities. And they have it better than anyone. They are living in a virtual state of bliss. They are happier than all of us."

"It's not right. People should know and have a choice. You are deciding for them."

"So now you want to decide for them instead? You take the Chip and that is what you are doing. You are deciding that their life now is not what they want and you will take it all away from them. Every day they have a choice. They choose to live within the society we have created. They want the luxuries New Europe provides. It was the choice to survive that built these walls."

"You have to give me the Chip," he pleads, not knowing what to think anymore. He just knew that he had to keep his part of the deal. Whatever happened after...

"Sorry, but I can't let you take it. I have seen what humans are capable of and it isn't something I want to see again." He closes his fist on the Chip and turns to leave.

A wall rises up in front of 3347, blocking his path. A sound of metal clanking together comes from where 3378 is standing. A sword appears in his hands, then it flashes, an electrical field surrounding it.

"What is this? How did you do that?" 3347 asks in astonishment.

"There is more to the outside world than your philosophies can dream of. Hand over the Chip and no one needs to get hurt."

"Don't make me kill you. I truly cared for you. But I will do what needs to be done to protect our world." A metal pole starts to form in his hands, sharp blades at either end. Even with his new protocols, 3378 knows this will be a hard fight to win and this is one of the people he would have chosen to save.

A wall appears in front of 3378 and he rolls to the right of it. A blade strikes at his head as he dodges and deflects it with his sword, the electricity making a spark as the weapons clash. The other end of the blade comes around and he ducks under it, stabbing at 3347's leg. The hit makes him stagger back. 3378 sees his opportunity and a wall shoots up under his feet, launching him into the air over 3347. 3347 raises his bar to deflect the attack, but he is too late. 3378 strikes down as he is over top of 3347, hitting the back of his shoulder. 3347 falls to the ground.

"It's over. Hand over the Chip."

"You'll have to pry it from my dead hands," 3347 says as he winces in pain.

"That's not what I want to do, but you leave me no choice."

"There's always a choice," he says, his speech laboured. 3378 steps closer and strikes at him again. 3347 blocks it from the ground. Another slash with the electrical sword crashes down on him, his block fading each time. "They won't let you leave. You can never get out."

"We'll see." 3378 raises his sword again. As he brings it down, he changes the path and slices 3347's wrist of the hand holding the Chip. 3347 screams out in pain, grabbing at his handless wrist. Grabbing the severed hand, 3378 opens it up and takes out the Chip. He creates a bandage and tie for 3347's arm and runs off with the Intel Chip.

Chapter 20

The door to the holding room closes, leaving 3347 lying on the floor, in pain, but still living. Down the hall, through the courtyard, back down the tunnel and out the water refuse. It was not far to go, but he knew he was being watched. If they sent 3347, they had to know it was him. They had all of the data on him from his Chip, his whole life uploaded to their processors. As he turns the corner, he hears a scream. "Nooooo," a woman's voice cries out. Through the windows in the hallway he can see a woman strapped to a platform. It is 9.

Through the glass walls he can see her in the courtyard, her arms and legs attached to a platform tilted on a 45-degree angle. He is not far from where he entered. If he kept going, he would make it out. He can see her make eye contact with him and she mouths the word "run". After a second of hesitation, he sends ten metal balls that smash through the window and jumps out after, glass exploding around him. He lands in the courtyard and runs towards 9.

From the corner of his eye he can see officers stationed on the top of the building, weapons trained on him. He sends up about 50 mini shields that float above him as the lasers begin to fly. Each shot is deflected by a shield as 3378 crouches under the cover and makes it to 9. He creates a dome around them to buy some time.

Making a pair of bolt-cutters, he snaps off the restraints holding her. "I told you to run! Now we are both screwed," she says with a tone of despair.

"You're welcome," he responds sarcastically.

"It was a trap. It was all a trap."

"The only way around a trap is to spring it. Just hold on."

"To what?"

The dome is surrounded by the officers, each closing in. He knows he has only a few seconds to get them both out of there. As the dome starts to fall, a blinding flash goes off and a loud bang right after. When the officers regain their sight, they see 3378 and 9 shoot into the air and glide out with long wooden wings attached to 3378's back. They take aim and fire at them in the sky, but they are too far for an accurate shot. The lasers hit the wings, which scorch them, but are not enough to bring them down. They can only watch as they glide over the wall.

On the other side, 3378 circles to an opening in the trees. He sets them down. "Are you okay?" he asks.

She whacks him hard with her hand. "You idiot! I told you to run…" She breaks down into sobs, falling to her knees, still hitting his legs with her fists.

"Hey, we don't have much time. Did anyone tell you anything?" He crouches down to her level, talking in as calm and soothing voice as he can. He knows they have maybe a minute before the pursuit is on them.

"Yes. It was one of the younger girls, I didn't recognize her. She said everything is not what it seems and that you would be coming. It wasn't long after that they grabbed me and chained me up."

"I'm going to take you somewhere different, but it is going to be tough getting out of here alive. I just need you to trust me," he begs, knowing it is the only hope of saving her. She doesn't say anything, she just nods her head, her sobs fading.

3378 starts to construct a two-person ITM, kind of an oxymoron he thinks. He also adds in a few mods as he goes, figuring some fire power might be necessary to get out in one piece. As the vehicle finishes the construction, he hears the drone of the officers' own vehicles in the distance. They both hop in and lift off as other ITMs appear just past the trees.

He could hear the police ITMs closing in behind him. Unfortunately, he didn't have time to get any special air maneuvering protocols, he would have to just wing this one. He lowers his ITM below the tree line, hoping they won't follow. His hopes are swiftly dashed as they all crash through the trees. He counts three by the sounds of their descent. Getting out of here might be harder than he thought.

He dodges trees left then right, narrowly missing the branches that are outstretched, arms of wood trying to catch him.

"You are going to have to fire at them. Grab the weapon controls," he yells back to 9.

"What? I can't. They'll arrest me!"

"Well they will most likely kill you if you don't."

"What have you dragged me into?" she asks as she picks up the controls from the ground. It is a rotary blaster similar to one she would have trained on before deployment.

"Hey, how did you get back to New Europe anyhow?"

"What? Ahhh," she screams as the first police ITM crashes through the brush to their right. She swings the weapon around and blasts wildly. It misses, but it is enough to throw the police vehicle off its course.

The second one slams into them from the left. 3378 pulls up hard to get out of the trees and evade another sideswipe. It works for a second, but all three are now in full sight above the foliage. "Blast them," he yells.

9 fires several shots, connecting on a few, but not inflicting enough damage to slow the pursuit.

"It's not working. They must have shields up or something," 9 shouts back.

"Plan B then."

"What's plan B?"

They drive back down into the trees. The three police follow them. "Shoot the trees down."

9 starts cutting down trees as they go. At first the vehicles are able to dodge around the falling branches, but 9 sees their pattern and starts changing the sides that she cuts down. The first vehicle dodges a falling tree to the left, but then two trees come from either side and it crashes into them, sending it to the ground. "One down, two to go," she calls to 3378.

The last two catch on to their strategy and pull up. For a moment, 3378 thinks they are in the clear. Suddenly, they both drop down on either side of them. They slam into them, pinching them and holding their course. They are headed straight for a large tree. 3378 jerks left and right, but he can't separate from either of them. "Hold on," he yells to 9.

He pulls up slightly, bringing both of them with him, then slams down, breaking free. The vehicles collide, one smashes into the tree and the other just grazes the edge, catching the top of its wing. 3378 watches as it spirals out of control.

While he is distracted, his ITM veers closer to the ground. "Look out!" 9 yells and 3378 pulls up inches away from the ground. As he does this, the last police ITM sees the opening and slams into them, sending them both hurtling towards the trees. They each ricochet off several trunks before grinding to a halt in the dirt.

For a few minutes everything is silent. For 3378, it all goes black.

***

"Get up, please!" The sound of 9's voice brings him back to reality. Things blur back into his vision.

"How long was I out?" he asks, blinking his eyes to try to focus. 9 wraps her arms around him. He can see the tears in her eye. This is the first affection she has shown him since their procreation years. And this was the first that seemed genuine.

"A few minutes longer than me. And I have no idea how long I was out," she says after she lets go.

"What about the police?"

"No sign of anything. I've heard a bunch flying overhead. They must have sent out the search parties. You really stepped on the hornet's nest this time," she says with a slight smile.

"We'll have to stay under cover then. We have a long way to go and we're running out of time."

"You must have something in your Chip that can get us there on the ground."

"Let me see what I can find," he says as he starts searching through the databases for old types of vehicles. He finds something that might work and begins constructing.

A wheel appears with a frame attached leading to a second wheel with a seat on top and a steering bar near the front wheel. He finds the protocol to operate this ancient motorized vehicle. "Hop on." He sits at the front and 9 sits behind him. "Grab my waist."

As she wraps her arms around him, he grabs the steering bar and rotates one handle. They drive five feet and fall over. "Are you okay?" he asks 9.

"That's two crashes in one day. Third time's a charm, right?"

"I can do this," he says, reprocessing the balancing protocol. This time they start out slow before he pulls his legs up. They start to speed up and he keeps them upright this time, leaning into the turns around the trees.

They can still hear the police ITMs scanning above the trees, but the growth is so thick, they are completely covered.

After a few hours of driving, they stop. The sun has gone down. "We'll have to stop here for the night. We should be safe to fly tomorrow," he tells 9, who looks ready to pass out right there.

He creates a small domed shelter for them to sleep in. 9 climbs in and closes her eyes, falling asleep instantly. 3378 looks at her sleeping for a minute before closing his own eyes. He has so many questions he wants to ask her, but he can't bring himself to wake her. She looks so peaceful and beautiful he thinks. He wishes the Chip could make him a time machine, then he could go back to the day he met her and change everything.

Chapter 21

3378 is running through the forest, the dark shadows of the trees grasping after him. He is searching for 9 but cannot find her. Suddenly he sees 42 stuck in a tree and motionless. He sees 9, but she is frozen in a tree as well. Then Eliza, the same, but with a giant hole in her. Then Alex is standing in his path, holding out his hand. 3378 moves closer to see what he is holding. As he closes in, he sees it is a tiny heart, slowly beating. He looks up and it is the sergeant from the battlefield in sector Y0W. The sergeant looks him in the eye and closes his hand into a fist, blood dripping through his clenched fingers. It smells like cooked meat.

3378 jumps out of his blankets, not sure where he is. The faint morning light trickles through the sleeping dome. 9 is not in her bed. He hears a snap outside. With a sudden sense of panic, he runs out of the dome.

Sitting at a fire is 9, roasting what looks like a small animal. "About time you got up. I thought you were in a hurry," she says to him casually, like they were on a weekend camping trip that humans used to do in the distant past.

"Sorry, I thought something happened to you. We do need to get going. We might already be too late."

"Well we have to eat first. We won't be good to anyone if we starve to death." The food did smell good and it reminded 3378 that it had been over a day since he last ate. He sits down beside 9 and she hands him a stick with some of the meat on it.

"How did you do all this?" 3378 asks.

"I might not have a fancy Chip, but mine still works and so does the rest of my body. You're not the only capable one here," she says with a tinge of spite.

"I didn't mean any offense. I've never hunted outside the walls before." He looks down at what he is eating. It looked about the size of a rabbit, but with tusks and six legs. "Is it safe to eat this?"

"Probably not, but we don't have much choice." He hears 3347's voice in his head; *you always have a choice.*

"Hey, you didn't get to tell me how you got back to New Europe. You were deployed when I was." He needed a few answers before they left. He trusted her, but he didn't trust those running New Europe.

"After you went off the grid, they brought me in for questioning. Because I was your procreation partner, they thought I would know everything about you."

"What did you tell them?"

"I told them the truth. You were just a regular guy like all the other 3000's." She smiled, but it still stung. "I also told them that you were caring and compassionate and took care of those who needed help. They took me back to New Europe and confined me to my quarters. Then when you came back they strapped me to that thing and used me as bait for you."

"Why did you warn me when we were sparring?"

"Because," she hesitates, looking away from him, "because I didn't want you to get hurt."

"What did you mean about something not being right here?"

"It's hard to explain. I have these memories and dreams and sometimes I can't tell which are real and which are not. Have you ever felt like you weren't in control? Like you were just watching your life? Like you weren't really you?" A tear pools in her eye and rolls down her cheek. He grabs her hand and she brushes the tear with her other.

He feels like there is more that she wants to say, but he doesn't press her. Instead, he says, "There is more to this world than you know. It's time to show you."

They finish eating in silence. 3378 creates a new two-person ITM. They climb in and lift off.

***

After a few hours of flying, they near sector V1E. In the distance they can see smoke and explosions. The assault has reached the interior base. It wouldn't be long before it was overrun.

They get as close as they can and land. They had made a plan on the trip. It wasn't the safest plan but it was the best they could come up with. As they got out, they each created deployment clothing and equipment, hoping they could blend in.

They made it to the back of the New Europe attack line. 3378 turns to 9 and says, "I want you to stay out of the fighting. I don't want you to get hurt again for me."

"For you? You think this is about you? First of all, I don't give a damn what you want. Second, you've almost killed me twice, so this should be safer. And third, I'm doing this whether you like it or not." The seriousness in her voice and face told him not to argue with her. In truth, he was always a little afraid of her.

When they reach the back of the lines, it is chaos. It appears that the defense is stronger than New Europe anticipated. Now to blend in with a squad. They rub dirt on their clothes to take the newly created look off.

They find a squad in disarray after a nearby explosion and move in. Several members are injured and they both start helping, figuring no one would question someone offering medical aid.

The first wounded soldier is missing a leg. He is screaming in pain and clutching his upper thigh, from the knee down has been blown to pieces. They both go in together. 9 tries to calm him down while 3378 starts addressing the wound. He quickly cleans out what he can, applies a cinching bandage and makes sure there is no more trauma. After they finish, they lie the soldier propped up behind the barricades. They tend to a few others before looking for an escape.

There is a lull in the fighting and 9 points to an open way, just one soldier is standing in the path, back to them. This may be their only opportunity. They head towards the soldier, keeping their heads down, hoping they go unnoticed.

"Where are you going?" sounds a booming voice, one that 3378 has heard before. Do they run or try to talk their way out of it? They both hesitate too long and slowly turn around. To 3378's horror, the voice belongs to the sergeant from the battle in sector YOW. 3378 wishes they had run. "What are your numbers and why are you not with your squad?"

"345 3360, sir. We have orders to infiltrate the base from these coordinates, sir." He hoped the sirs would make it sound official. Hope was running out.

"345 3360 was KIA and no orders to infiltrate the base have been given. You have two seconds to convince me not to execute you right now," he spits out as he pulls out his weapon.

3378 remembers the story of Ajax, Hector, and Odysseus. In the split second he recalls the sacrifice of the Greek soldiers for something more than themselves. With that thought he acts. The sergeant is sent flying back into the air, at least 30 feet high. They both stare for a second, shocked by what just happened. 9 grabs 3378's arm and they both run towards the base entrance. They bought a few minutes of time, but they also brought on the wrath of the sergeant.

Chapter 22

As they enter the base, Alex is in the hallway, waiting for them. "Seize the girl. We don't know who she is." Two soldiers move towards her.

"Wait! She is with me. You can trust her," 3378 pleads, putting his hand up to the soldiers.

"Unfortunately we can't take that risk in the middle of a war and we don't have time to run the diagnostics." They move in and grab 9.

3378 holds up the Intel Chip held between his fingers. "If you touch her, this gets destroyed!"

"Just calm down, don't do anything rash," Alex says in a soothing voice. "We can work this out. We all want the same thing."

"Do we?" This was the first time he had really challenged Alex and all that he stood for. "What is it exactly that you want?"

"A world where everyone has a fair chance! A world where outcasts don't have to live in fear! A world where humans can be free! And with every second we waste, the dream of that world fades." The anger was showing through the colour in his face.

"Yes, I do want all that and the thing enslaving people is THIS!" he yells, showing the Chip again for emphasis. "With this gone, no more facilities, no more fighting, no more power." For once, he finally felt in control of the situation. The look on Alex's face told him that he had the upper hand.

He had risked his life to bring this Chip here and now he was going to destroy it. What would happen if he did? Was this really the right decision? Would it really change anything?

Alex makes a move towards 3378 and everything after happens almost instantaneously. A wall shoots up in front of Alex, 3378 side kicks one soldier and 9 ducks as a laser shoots at the soldier holding her. Alex is on the ground, looking up at 3378, tears of defeat in his eyes.

"No one should have such power. I should have had my Chip taken out when I had the chance. But now I can make a choice that will help others. It starts with this," 3378 says as he crushes the Chip in his hand. Alex's head sinks, knowing that with this action, his last hopes die as well.

The base starts to shake from the explosions outside. "Come on, we can still get out of here alive," 3378 says to Alex, offering his hand. Alex looks at him, grabs his hand and pulls him to the ground.

"It is over for us and for you too," he yells, holding 3378 to the ground. A chunk of the wall breaks off and crashes to the ground next to them. 9 screams and runs to 3378, but a barrier springs up between them.

"Get out!" 3378 yells to her. "Don't worry about me." He hears her yelling and pounding the wall, then another crash. There is a second of silence then he can hear her footsteps slowly fading as she heads for the exit. Now how is he going to get himself out? Alex has his arm around his neck, if he does anything to Alex, he risks it hitting him too.

The other side of the room starts to crumble. He gets an idea. A platform forms beneath them and sends them upwards, slamming them both into the roof. It stuns both of them but loosens Alex's hold on him. Luckily, he was still wearing his helmet from blending in with the soldiers. 3378 slowly gets to his feet. Alex lies motionless next to him. He grabs Alex under his arms and throws him over his shoulder. It is a heavy load, but he doesn't have far to go.

As he gets to the tunnel out, he stands Alex straight up beside him. There is no way he could carry him up the ladder and there is not much time left to get out. The base is quickly filling with rubble from the fallen walls. Soon everything will start to collapse.

He holds onto Alex tight, so that they could both squeeze through the opening. A column starts to rise under their feet and continues to rise as they ascend towards the light.

When they make it to the top, he drops Alex on the ground. 9 is there and so are twenty New European soldiers, their weapons aimed at them. Two soldiers move apart to let the sergeant through. A stream of blood has dried down the side of his face and he moves with a limp. He looks directly at 3378.

As they enter the base, Alex is in the hallway, waiting for them. "Seize the girl. We don't know who she is." Two soldiers move towards her.

9 gets ready to fight, but 3378 steps in front of her and holds his hand up to the soldiers. They hesitate for a second and that is all 3378 needs to send them flying backwards with an angled column under their feet.

"Hold on now, we are on your side," Alex says, turning to see that the soldiers are still conscious. They slowly start to get up, clearly dazed by the force of being thrown.

"Are you?" 3378 asks. "What is it that you really want?"

"I want everyone to have what you have had your whole life."

"What if that isn't possible? How do you think we got to this point?"

"So the few lucky ones get everything while the rest suffer?" Alex counters.

The building starts to shake from the explosions outside. The soldiers are back on their feet and look ready to return the favour. They draw their guns and aim them at 3378. Footsteps start to sound from outside of the room.

"We don't have much time. Give me the Intel Chip and we can all get out of here. We can make things better," Alex pleads, holding out his hand.

The footsteps get louder and 3378 turns around to see a wall of New European soldiers standing inside the entrance. He turns back to Alex to see the look of desperation in his eyes. There is no winner in this game he thinks.

With guns pointed at him from both sides, he grabs 9 around the waist and uses a catapult to launch them over the New European soldiers and out of the base. It catches them by surprise and they just stare as they fly over their heads.

An ITM starts to form around them as they glide past the soldiers who are now aiming their guns at them. The ITM wall forms in time to deflect their bullets. 3378 lets go of 9 and maneuvers around to fit into the control seat, 9 squeezing in behind him. Regular ITMs weren't designed to hold passengers, but one could fit in an emergency.

The ITM slams into the ground, sending 3378 and 9 into the side. Bullets ricochet off the exterior. 3378 knows the shields won't hold for long. He grabs the controls and pulls up. The ITM jumps to life and blasts off the ground, dodging the barrage of fire from behind.

"What now?" 9 asks quietly, still feeling the effects from slamming into the ground.

"Now? Now we stay alive."

Everything starts to flicker. Then it all goes black.

As they enter the base, Alex is in the hallway, waiting for them. "Seize the girl. We don't know who she is." Two soldiers move towards her.

3378 sends up two barriers, blocking off the soldiers. "She stays with me or there is no Chip," 3378 says in his most commanding voice.

"Okay, okay, just hand me the Chip," Alex says, his hands out. 3378 moves forward and drops the Chip in his hands. "Thank you. We don't have much time left, but we can still make it out. Follow me."

They all run down the hall, following Alex. They take the stairs downwards. The base shakes as the explosions continue to rain down above ground. "Shouldn't we be going up?" 3378 asks.

"Not if we want to stay alive after we get out," Alex responds as they continue to descend. They turn a corner and another before they enter a large room. It appears to be some sort of hangar with a few flying vehicles from the 25th century. Alex motions for them to climb into one as he runs to one of the men. 3378 can barely hear him say, "Start the evacuation," before he gets in the ship.

It is not as comfortable or spacious as the LGTs, but it can fit them all. The large door to the hangar opens, revealing an exit large enough for each flying vehicle in the hangar. Part of the wall crashes to the floor on the far side of the hangar. 3378 can hear the alarm going off as people start streaming into the hangar and onto the ships.

Alex powers up their vehicle and lights flash on all around them. The hangar doors open completely, and they lift off the ground and glide through the opening. 3378 looks out the back to see an opening in the side of a cliff and several other ships follow out after them.

Fire from the ground begins to erupt around them as the soldiers change their targets to the escaping vehicles. They know they have won the battle and want to finish the war. Their goal is to wipe out all outsiders.

The ship makes a clean escape, but several others are brought down in the barrage. They caught the New European army by surprise and they are too far from their LGTs to catch them, but a pursuit would be inevitable.

The remaining ships set down after over an hour of flying, changing course several times to buy some much needed time. As they exit the ship, 3378 is amazed by the sight. It is a triangular prism shaped structure with a small opening. It is perfectly symmetrical, except for a chunk missing from the side to the left of the opening. 3378 had never seen anything like this in his life. How could such things exist without him knowing about it?

Inside the structure, there is a large room filled with different forms of technology and people moving all around, methodically working on something. Alex leads 3378 into the middle of the room and turns towards him, "This is the main command center. Where we were was the last major outpost. We have a few other smaller ones, but nothing big enough to mount a counter attack. If they hit us here, we will be all but wiped out."

"So what's the plan now?" 3378 asks, slightly worried by the possible answers.

"Now we gather every weapon and able body we have to form an army to attack New Europe. With the Intel Chip, we can start making our own Chips. We won't have many, but hopefully it will be enough to give us an advantage."

"But who will take them? Any adults will die."

"Yes, but not right away. We have many volunteers already waiting. They know the sacrifice they make is for a better world. They have lived in oppression their whole lives and are willing to do whatever it takes to end it."

"What about me? I held up my end of the bargain. Am I free to go?"

"Yes, you are free, however, we need someone to lead this army."

"What? Me?"

"You know New Europe better than anyone. You can do things with your Chip that no one else can. You have come this far, don't you want to see it through to the end?"

It had never occurred to him that he would be asked to lead an army against his own home, his own people. But did he really know what that home was? A home that was ready to turn him into a mindless slave because of one minor infraction? Almost everyone he cared about was out of New Europe or dead. What was it that he was fighting for? Other people were willing to give their life for this cause. Was he?

Chapter 23

"What if we try having the girl die in battle before he meets Alex? That seems to be a sticking point," a man in a black blazer says to a woman in a white lab coat.

"No, it's useless. We need to just scrap this case and start all over. We had more success with the earlier versions. This one just won't break as easily. We can't pin our hopes on such fluctuations in the testing."

"But look at the resilience and creativity. These traits could prove valuable in extreme situations, which are sure to arise."

"Well we are running these tests to minimize the chances for those *extreme situations*. The gusto shown by this case is exactly what we are trying to root out. How can we build a society that will survive if there are those that will turn on themselves?"

"I see your point. We can't have random cowboys running off and starting revolutions, but there has to be a way to keep them committed to the greater good of society without losing their autonomy."

"That is the paradox. How do you control something and give it autonomy? We can increase the amount of influence the Chip has on the individuals, but then are they really human? This is the society we are going to be living in. Do we want to be surrounded by robots?"

"No, but it is human nature to resist and fight. You can see it at every obstacle in the simulation." The man in the blazer turns his back to the woman and walks to the edge of the room. He looks down at a miniature version of New Europe, with tiny people moving inside. "Perhaps the problem is humanity itself."

"What are you suggesting?" the woman in the lab coat asks, incredulity in her voice.

"I'm suggesting maybe this is not the right species. Maybe we need to look somewhere else."

"How many more planets do we need to visit before you realize that this is our best option? There is nothing with such grace and intelligence in any of the systems we have been through. Yes, there is pain and suffering, but that is why we are doing the testing. Look at how far we have come. Remember when we were at 1 and we thought we would never finish? Now we are on 445 3378! Each day we get closer.”

The man in the blazer turns back towards the woman. “I’m sorry. I just long to be back. It has been a tiring journey.”

“I know. This will work. A couple of changes to the algorithms and a few extra tests and we should have it. We’ll scrap this case, but most of the others we can keep.” She moves closer the man, touching his hand. “This is where we will live. It won’t be perfect, but it will be life and we will be together.”

Epilogue

3378 steps out of the simulator. It is a faint whisper, but one that he can hear clearly now. It is a girl's voice, soft but certain. All of his dreams, his memories are starting to come together. Now he knows the choice he has to make. Now he knows that he can make it. The sweet timbre is like a solace to him now, "You have to get away."

www.ingramcontent.com/pod-product-compliance
Lightning Source LLC
Chambersburg PA
CBHW070519200726
48293CB00007B/2593